Just A Job

Patsy Collins

To everyone I've ever worked with –
for many and varied reasons.

Contents

1. Unfriending Moira

"You'll like this one," Lynsey said showing me her phone.

I smiled at the picture of a sleepy looking owl and its caption of 'soooo not a morning person'.

Lynsey is a nice kid. She lives next door and we get the same bus; me to work, her to college. She's always tapping away on that phone of hers. Talking to her Facebook friends she says, but she chats to me at the same time and sometimes finishes off her homework as well. We often laugh at things her friends have 'posted'. Although I rarely 'LOL' (Laugh Out Loud) I often chuckle.

"What do you think of this, Jean?" She showed me a picture of a lovely sweater her friend had made. As I admired it I wondered if the other girl could simultaneously knit and chat on Facebook.

"She has a real talent," I said.

"Yeah, she's brills at all kinds of craft stuff and starting up a small business making things to order."

Then Lynsey got into an animated discussion about a television programme. She fired off replies so fast I couldn't see her fingers move over the tiny keypad, until I nudged her to let her know we were close to her stop. She snapped her phone shut, so she wouldn't get distracted and miss it again.

"It's not like real life," I told her. "Facebook friends aren't like real friends."

"Yeah they are, they're real. Laters!" Then she was gone.

She was wrong, I thought. My friend Moira for example; I

bet Lynsey's Facebook friends aren't like her. Gosh that woman is annoying! She has grandchildren and you'd think she was the only woman in the world who'd managed it. Everything is turned round to them. I ask how she is, she tells me about their teething or measles. Mention any kind of food and she tells me if they like it or not. I do understand her interest in them, I'd love some of my own but I don't keep on about it.

"Argh! Give me a break!" Lynsey said a few days later.

"What's up?"

"My friend who does the craftwork? She turns every conversation to it. If someone says there's a birthday coming up she says she makes gift items. If she posts a picture she's always wearing something she made and says so. If anyone posts a picture of themselves she says how nice they'd look in her crocheted tops …"

"Maybe I was wrong about Facebook friends not being like real ones," I admitted.

Last week one of our colleagues expressed an interest in going to the Lake District. Moira said she'd been and would bring in some photos. Of course they were all of the grandkids. If we were lucky we caught a glimpse of the lovely scenery over their shoulders. All the advice she had for things to do was centred round what the grandkids had enjoyed. Was I the only one who saw it was of no interest to our young colleague who was going away with her boyfriend? Why didn't anyone tell Moira to shut up about the grandchildren?

"I've totally had it with her! I'm unfriending her," Lynsey said the next day.

Apparently the craft person had posted a picture of a day at the zoo and held up her clothes in such a way that the animals all seemed to be wearing, or at least admiring, them. The first couple were quite clever, I thought, but towards the end of the bus journey I'd had quite enough of them. I could see why Lynsey was irritated and said so.

"It's not so much the pictures, but she's asking everyone to share her posts and help promote her stuff for her. I'm really fed up. There, done!"

Lynsey explained that with a few clicks she could unfriend a person and need never see their irritating posts or hear from them again.

"So I was right the first time," I said. "Reality isn't like Facebook because I can't just unfriend Moira."

Actually I was wrong again. Moira asked me to take part in some sponsored thing for her grandchildren's school. Not give her a couple of pounds I don't mean, but actually take part. I was expected to go round all my friends and neighbours asking them to pay out money for something I didn't even particularly want to do. We had a huge row; a real unfriending.

Lynsey paid much more attention to me on the bus the next day. It was nice to talk to someone who didn't have their own agenda and I flattered myself she felt the same way.

The following week was quiet. It was half term so Moira was off work looking after the grandchildren, which was rather a relief. It was half term for Lynsey too and by the end of the week I was feeling a bit lonely.

Well, not exactly lonely, but I was desperate for someone to talk to. I'd had some wonderful news and longed to share it. I did tell my colleagues, the neighbours and anyone else who'd listen, but it's not the same as sharing with a real friend, is it?

On Monday Lynsey congratulated me with her usual half attention. I'd spent the weekend knitting, but even without that I'd have remarked on Lynsey's wonderful sweater.

"Fab innit? My friend made it."

"The unfriended one?"

"Yeah, I've re-friended her now. She sent me an email saying she saw I'd unfriended her and was it a mistake? So I explained why I'd done it and she apologised. Said that after having a few sales she was excited and just got a bit carried away."

"I can see how that could happen." I could. Work colleagues and neighbours were beginning to get a patient look on their faces whenever I started talking.

Moira and I exchanged an icily polite, "Good morning." How I wished there were buttons I could press to re-friend her.

There were; Moira discovered them first. She sent me an email on the office computer. *Heard your Christine is expecting. Congratulations.*

Thank you, I typed back, adding :-) as Lynsey had taught me, in the hopes of showing how pleased I was.

Want to talk about it? Moira replied.

Poor woman didn't get a word in the whole lunchtime, but I know she'll forgive me; she's a real friend.

2. Water!

Martin staggers forward, his feet sinking into the hot sand. The heat shimmers off the nearest dunes, giving the impression of sparkling pools, reminding him of the water he so urgently needs. His eyes are stinging from the sweat that constantly runs into them. Desperately he reaches for the map he'd been given. He prays the map is right, because he doesn't have the strength to go much further.

Last night, stray dogs stole his food. He could live without the food, but they'd also ripped a hole in his last container of water. He knows he cannot continue to follow the trail. It will take him two days to reach the next settlement. Martin doesn't know how long he can survive in the desert without water; doesn't want to know. Staring into the distance, he sees a building. He hopes it truly is Nessim's Hotel, not a delusion produced by the heat and his eager imagination.

When he'd booked this trip, he hadn't expected to be doing this. He booked the holiday on impulse after seeing the offer advertised in a travel agent's window. It had sounded like an adventure. In Egypt, he could visit pyramids and fantastic tombs. Maybe he would sail down the Nile. He'd soon got disillusioned. His hotel was miles from the historic sights. This was just a standard beach holiday and no fun on his own. He'd wanted more than to just sit, alone, at a bar or lie on a sunbed, so when he'd learnt of this optional excursion he'd instantly decided to go. Walking across an Egyptian desert had seemed such a romantic idea. Of course, he couldn't walk across a real desert, but he could wander the arid region that separated the shifting sands from civilisation. There were adequately marked tracks, used by local traders. He was pleased he could still remember how to use a compass. Perhaps those work's team-building trips hadn't been a complete waste of time after all. All the settlements he would travel through had places he could buy food and water, he'd been assured. There were even hotels where he could stay for a comfortable night's sleep.

After five days, he'd discovered that here, at the fringe of the desert, nothing was as it seemed. The food was never anything more palatable than dried goats meat or dusty, tasteless nuts. The water was always cloudy and tasted awful, yet cost the same as the finest champagne. The hotels were wooden huts, with tin roofs. The better ones had camp beds and a clean blanket. The more usual offering was a greasy sleeping bag on the floor. He shook his boots each morning to remove any creatures that might lurk there. Previously Martin had never bothered too much about personal cleanliness. He shaved and washed because it was expected of him. Now he longed to stand under a shower and remove the sweat and dust that filled his pores.

Martin had thought the desert would be exciting, but all he'd seen was sand. Even the few things that were not sand were so bleached and dry they might as well have been. The sand was in his shoes, his clothes. It had worked its way into his ears and up his nose. There was sand trapped under the frames of the sunglasses that pressed into his skin, rubbing it raw. He was sure that his sweat was becoming thicker, more concentrated. It no longer poured out of him, but oozed, coating his skin in a suffocating layer.

It occurred to him that he must either walk for five days

back, or continue with the journey. Pride made him decide to see it through. Gradually he'd begun to see the journey as a positive thing. It couldn't really be called fun, but at least he was doing something different. Back at the office people would actually listen to his holiday story. They might even be slightly impressed. He'd be slimmer and fitter too. His doctor had told him to cut down on the fat and alcohol and get more exercise. He was doing all that – and some!

On the sixth day, he'd reached a slightly larger group of buildings. The locals called it a town. Martin didn't think it even qualified as a village. He'd seen a sign for a restaurant; not expected anything close to his idea of that. He was pleasantly surprised. He'd eaten his first proper meal for days. How good the vegetables had tasted! Never before had he enjoyed eating something he knew to be good for him. Although beer and spirits were on offer he'd drank glass after glass of clear, cool water; amazed how refreshing it was. He'd asked the shop owner if there was a hotel he could stay in for the night. There had been no luxurious facilities, just another hut, with an earth floor.

The shop owner's son had run after him as he left in the morning and given him a leaflet.

"My uncle's hotel, very nice, you visit," the boy had said.

Martin had seen that, as well as an advertisement for Nessim's Hotel, the leaflet was a map of the region. He'd kept it as a souvenir.

The next night he'd stayed in the dirtiest hut yet and lost his food and water. He'd refused to buy more from the man who'd allowed wild dogs to rob him as he slept.

Now perhaps the map can save his life. He studies it carefully and sets off in what, as far as he can judge, is the right direction. Soon he sees a building, in the place marked by the map.

The heat haze makes it difficult to see clearly. At times, he can see nothing. At others, he sees a large square structure, which could indeed be a hotel. At last, he reaches it. He has no strength to knock on the panelled door.

"Water, sir?" a voice asks.

Martin nods. His dry lips and swollen tongue cannot form words.

"Still, or sparkling?" the voice asks. Martin looks up and sees a tall man, smartly dressed in a dark suit. He holds a gleaming silver tray. On the tray are a crystal goblet, bowls of ice and sliced citrus fruit. There is a pair of silver tongs.

"Ice and a twist of lemon?" the hotel keeper asks.

A mirage. Just a mirage.

Martin staggers on. Just yards ahead a ragged man runs out. He offers a rusty canteen. Gratefully Martin drinks the stale, evil tasting, water. He pays the man very generously for more water and some sand-covered slivers of dried goat's meat. Martin continues his journey with a new respect for the desert, and himself.

Behind him, Mr Nessim stands and watches. This happens so often. After seeing him and his clean hotel with delicious food and refreshing drinks, the weary traveller does not believe the evidence of his own eyes and turns away. The hotel keeper shrugs. It doesn't matter to him; the man now has enough food and water to safely continue his journey, and Mr Nessim has made a nice profit.

Things are often not what they seem, in the desert. Martin hadn't noticed Mr Nessim throw off his smart suit and polished shoes before coming after him with a new, perhaps more believable, offer of help.

3. Just A Job

It was 3am on Lister Ward. That's when the patients were usually asleep and we could talk. We talked about anything, dates, diets, shoes, astrology. Well, Pattie and I talked; Michelle's a bit shy, she just listens usually. That night, we were actually talking about work. Pattie had started it by asking why we'd each become nurses and if we thought nursing was a noble calling or just a job.

"It was a sick little girl I saw one day, made me decide," Pattie explained.

Michelle twisted her hair in her hands; the way she did when she was nervous.

"Nobody helped; they didn't even seem to notice her," Pattie continued. "I was just a kid myself, wasn't nothing I could do. I decided whenever someone needed me in future I wouldn't be so helpless."

"So you trained as a nurse?" I asked. It was hard to picture big, dark capable Sister Pattie Rohorne, as a helpless child.

"Yes. As a poor South African kid things weren't easy but I worked hard, got a scholarship. The rest is history," Pattie said, grinning and smoothing down the skirt of her immaculate uniform.

I thought Michelle was going to speak, but she just looked at me as though hoping I'd say something.

"I'm not sure why I drove down to the sea wall that day," I said. "I was fed up, but not so depressed I intended to keep going until all that was left was an oily smear on the surface. It was dark, with a bitterly cold wind. That's when I saw her."

"Saw who?" Michelle asked. She sounded as though something was bothering her.

"Just some kid; she didn't have a coat. I didn't notice her until she'd gone by; I saw her in the mirror. I turned the car round to go after her. That took a while, it's narrow down there."

"Slippery too, it's surprising no one's gone in. They haven't have they?" asked Michelle.

"Not as far as I know. Anyway, once I'd turned round, I started having second thoughts. She might think I was some kind of weirdo and have me arrested," I said.

"Nobody would believe that surely? You're great with kids. How's your niece by the way?" asked Michelle. She looked as though I'd said something out of line and I was sure she was trying to change the subject.

"Fine. What's up?"

She just shrugged and shook her head.

"I was upset, I'd failed my driving test that afternoon," I continued.

"But you were driving." Pattie obviously disapproved.

"Yes. After the test, Dad presented me with car keys. He'd bought me a red mini. It never occurred to him I wouldn't pass and I felt such a failure I couldn't explain. I'd been struggling with my schoolwork too. My parents wanted me to go to university, so I was doing A levels. They thought nursing was just a passing fancy and I felt I was letting them down. I said I wanted to go for a drive on my own."

"But the girl?" whispered Michelle. She was fiddling with

her hair again.

"I decided to just drive up and down, keeping an eye on her. I thought she'd either go into a house and be fine, or I could stop in the road opposite and ask if she wanted help."

We were interrupted by a patient who'd pressed his buzzer.

"My turn," said Michelle almost leaping off her stool. She seemed anxious; I wondered if she knew something about the girl and hoped she wasn't going to tell me anything bad had happened to her.

"What happened to the little South African girl?" I asked Pattie, to distract myself.

"I don't know, I never saw her again. I just saw her the once, walking through the market place, all alone."

"What was wrong with her?"

"Don't know that either. Just knew she was sick. Mother laughed and said not to worry, all white folks look sick."

Michelle came back; the patient was in a lot of pain. Pattie prepared a morphine injection. Whilst she did, Michelle and I performed the routine observations of patients who needed them, quietly checking pulses and temperatures. The other patients were comfortable, most asleep. When we returned to our station, Pattie had made tea. Well, it was nearly an hour since our last cup.

"So, what did happen to your little girl?" Pattie asked.

"I couldn't find her. A couple of times I thought I caught a glimpse of her yellow dress behind a parked car, or in my mirror. When I turned she was gone. I panicked. I'd known something wasn't right the moment I saw her. She was too young."

"Little children shouldn't be out in the cold on their own,

but you knew that already," Pattie pointed out.

Michelle had wrapped her hair so tightly around her hand that her fingers were white.

"She was the same age as when I'd seen her years before."

Neither of them seemed to think it odd I'd seen her previously.

"I remembered visiting my grandfather in hospital. He'd had a stroke. My mother went every day and took me too. I hated it, I was frightened of all the sick old people. They made such horrible noises."

"They still do," Pattie reminded us.

"Yeah, but at least now I understand, have a chance of helping them. I couldn't do anything then. Anyway, Mum let me go and sit in the garden and read a book. Sometimes there was this little girl walking by in a fancy yellow dress. The first time I saw her I thought she was a visitor, like me."

"Which hospital was it?" Michelle interrupted.

"This one," I said, wondering what was up with Michelle.

"Anyway, I felt sorry for her because her mum had made her get all dressed up. My hair was as long as hers, but Mum hadn't made me have ringlets and big blue bows. My gingham dress and headband suddenly didn't seem so bad. I took a bit more notice the next time and realised she was really sick. She was so thin and pale she hardly seemed to be there at all."

"Did you speak to her?" asked Michelle. The question sounded like an accusation.

"No. It didn't seem right. I didn't see her again. Somehow I knew she hadn't got better."

"You thought she'd died?" Pattie asked.

"I'm not sure I was old enough to work that out. Anyway after that Grandfather started getting better. He could talk properly again. I was less scared of the hospital. I made cards for everyone on his ward. They told me it made them feel better, so I decided I wanted to be a nurse."

"You think the girl by the sea wall was the same one?" said Pattie.

"I did, but that's impossible. This one was the same age, only it was ten years later," I said.

"Did you find her?"

"No, but my dad found me. He'd got worried, thought I'd had an accident. I was in a bit of a state and begged him to help me look for the girl. He asked which car we should use. I told him his, as I shouldn't be driving. As we searched I managed to tell him about failing my test."

"Was he angry?" asked Pattie.

"No, he stopped the car to hug me. 'That's my girl,' he said 'took me three goes, and there was me thinking you'd do better and pass first time.' It was then he realised I'd felt under pressure to pass. We had quite a chat and I explained I really did want to be a nurse; it wasn't just a childhood dream. Like Pattie said, it's all history after that."

"You didn't find the girl?" Michelle said, leaning toward me. She definitely knew something.

"No. We did look, but she must have got home safely in the end."

"Where was the last place you saw her?" asked Michelle.

"Right outside this hospital."

"She was home then," said Michelle.

"You know who she was?" I asked. I wasn't sure I wanted to hear the answer.

"Palest blue eyes you ever saw, long blonde hair, in huge ringlets tied with blue ribbons. Long flounced primrose yellow dress, and a sash to match the bows in her hair. Dainty brown boots. Sound familiar?"

"But that's the girl from the market," Pattie said.

"That's her. That's the girl I saw. Michelle, what does this mean?" I demanded. Things were getting weird

"I've seen her too. I was fifteen and set to run away with the circus."

"No!"

"Near enough. Actually, I planned to go off with a young man who worked the dodgems from the visiting fair. I'd packed a bag and sneaked out at night. He was going to pick me up on the main road."

She must have noticed Pattie and I staring then, as she blushed. I wondered what could have changed a wild irresponsible girl into a quiet sensible nurse.

"The girl walked past, going in the opposite direction. She stood outside my house and waited. I don't know why but I walked back. When I reached her, she pointed towards the house. I went in and found my brother having a fit. He'd fallen over a glass coffee table and was badly cut too. I called the ambulance then woke my parents."

"Then you decided to become a nurse, and the rest is history?" Pattie suggested.

"I didn't decide that night, but a few days later we had to choose somewhere to do our work experience. I came here," Michelle told us.

"Not this actual ward?" I asked.

"No, Curie Ward. I saw her picture there. It's still in the hospital, perhaps you'd like to see it?"

We were busy then with the next set of observations. The blood pressure and temperature readings were taken as quickly and quietly as possible. Getting back to sleep in a hospital bed isn't always easy, so we prefer not to wake patients whenever possible. Two people did wake up, and as is usual, they then asked to be taken to the toilet. By the time everyone was settled, our shift was almost over. All that remained for us to do was prepare a brief for the staff who'd relieve us and ensure we'd cleared away any mess from our tea breaks.

"Do you want to see that picture now?" Michelle asked immediately we left the ward.

We did of course. Michelle led us down corridors and through automatic doors. None of us spoke. We walked over brick pathways and under dark archways, the echoes of our footsteps were the only sound. Even the sea was quiet. It felt as if we were the only people in the hospital. I kept close to the others. We climbed stairs and entered an empty waiting room. We walked past the empty rows of orange plastic chairs and stopped outside a consulting room. Michelle ushered us in before turning on the light. We saw a large framed poster. It was slightly faded but we all recognised those pale blue eyes, blonde ringlets and frilly yellow dress. There was a speech bubble, 'I'm sick, please come and make me well'. Underneath was the caption, 'Nursing – a noble vocation, not just a job.'

"I saw this whilst doing my work experience," said Michelle. "As you can imagine it made quite an impression on me. I asked about it. Dr Gaskin is interested in local history and did some research. It turns out this was intended as a recruitment poster. It was never used, but I think you'll agree it has been effective."

4. Making The Right Impression

"What's wrong with me, Mum?" Jenna asked.

"Nothing at all, love. Why would you think there was?"

"I'm still single."

"Nothing wrong with that. Plenty of women …"

"I know, I know," Jenna interrupted. "There's nothing wrong with being single by choice, but it's not what I want."

"Fair enough, but I still don't think you should be fretting over it. You're young yet. You'll meet the right man soon enough."

Her sister, Hilary, said much the same.

Dad wasn't any more help. "You're perfect, love, inside and out. Any man would be lucky to have you."

Trouble was, no men seemed to agree. Most seemed uncomfortable in her presence. Even her young nephew, Liam, clammed up when Jenna was around.

Jenna needed to know what was wrong, so she could she put things right. She couldn't ask for advice in the office. Tom worked there.

Her friends just laughed and told her not to be silly. "You're great, just as you are, Jenna."

"Maybe you should try not to seem too desperate," was the most sensible reply she got. That wasn't so easy to do; she was desperate. Tom, the only man she knew who seemed able to hold a conversation with her, was leaving the company in less than a month.

She was sure her favourite magazine would offer reliable, impartial advice. It did. There were articles to help her lose weight, gain energy, or for increasing her confidence and happiness. They weren't what she needed. Jenna was already fit, healthy and the right weight for her height. She had a job she quite liked, good friends and a supportive family. She had plenty of interests and very little stress; except where Tom was concerned.

Jenna often found herself correcting Tom's work. Sometimes there was a spelling mistake in an important report, or a figure not rounded up correctly. She'd stopped pointing out these errors, as he didn't seem to think they mattered much, but couldn't bring herself to present work she knew to be less than perfect.

She couldn't think of a way to move their relationship on from that of friendly colleagues. Tom smiled whenever he saw her, always said 'hello'. He watched her sometimes as she worked at her computer. He held doors open and was always there when she needed help to carry anything. He'd even taken her for a drink once. Just once.

Jenna tried a new look. Over the weekend she updated her entire wardrobe. She arrived at work looking as though she'd stepped out of a fashion magazine, rather than into a rather conventional office. The girls gushed over her stylish outfit.

Tom blinked, then greeted her just as usual. Jenna knew she didn't look any better than she had done in her more appropriate, classic clothes.

Jenna had her hair coloured and shortened. The result was a sleek bob in eye catching, glistening red. It looked good, but then so had her naturally honey-blonde flowing locks. The girls at work raved about her new style.

Tom blinked twice, then said 'hello'.

"You're trying too hard," Mum said. "People like you for who you are, not your hair or clothes."

Maybe Mum was right. Even Tom seemed uncomfortable around her these days.

"Why don't you try to relax a bit?" her friends suggested.

"A complete break from routine, that's what you need," her sister said.

"Do you think so?"

"Sure. Take a day off work and do something different. Give this Tim a chance to miss you."

Hilary had Tom's name wrong and the main reason she wanted Jenna to take time off work was her hope she'd take Hilary's sulky son out for the day. That didn't mean she was wrong.

Liam wanted to roller skate and persuaded her to visit the outdoor rink. Jenna discovered she'd need socks, so her smart outfit was accessorised by a schoolboy's football ones. She broke a nail lacing the boots and a few spots of rain soon turned her smooth bob into a blob of frizz.

That was all forgotten though when she fell and ripped her blouse, exposing one shoulder and a generous portion of cleavage. Her nephew didn't accept that as a valid reason to stop. Instead, it provided him with an excuse to take her hand and whiz her around the rink at great speed.

Jenna wasn't entirely sure if she was crying from alarm or if the tears were of laughter, but she was pretty sure they were smearing mascara down her cheeks.

"I'll help you, Aunty Jenna," he promised as he demonstrated how to stop and caught her when she failed to master the technique.

She'd never seen him so happy. "You really like skating, don't you?"

"Yes. I'm good at it." To prove his point, he whirled away, span in a neat circle, leapt into the air, landed perfectly and raced back to stop dead, just inches in front of her. "Rubbish at everything else, but great at skating."

She tried to say he wasn't rubbish at anything, but he was still talking.

"You, on the other hand are brilliant at everything and that's pretty scary."

"I'm rubbish at skating," Jenna pointed out.

"Yeah. I like you loads better now I know that."

"You do?"

"Yeah. When I grow up, I want a girlfriend just like you."

The one time Tom had taken her out, he'd complimented her on her looks, her efficiency at work, her ability to deal with any situation. She'd revealed she could speak French, had passed her driving test at the first attempt and was an accomplished cook. Perhaps all that was a bit intimidating?

"So why did you want to come out with me today, if you thought I was scary?"

"Because you're nice as well and I wanted to show you I was good at something."

Tom must have thought she was nice, or he wouldn't have asked her out. He hadn't done anything to impress her though.

Liam took a photo of her with his phone.

"What are you going to do with that?" she asked.

"Put it up on my Facebook wall."

Tomorrow, Jenna could arrive at work without the perfect

makeup, with a few hairs out of place and make a spelling mistake in one of her reports. Instead of working diligently she could log into Facebook and let Tom see the picture of her looking dishevelled and approachably incompetent.

She could, or she could sign Tom's leaving card, wish him well and go back to being herself. Mum was right, there wasn't anything wrong with her; the issue was with the men she'd so far encountered.

To be happy, she needed to share her life with someone who had skills of his own and who wasn't intimidated by her talents. Tom wasn't that man.

5. The Syndicate

I never wanted to do it, but I was made to run the lottery syndicate. Why on earth was I asked? My filing is disorganised, I'm always forgetting important things and since I started this, I've dreaded the day disaster strikes.

Sophie engineered it.

"Marie should do it, she's so good with people I'm sure she would love to be asked," I heard her saying to our boss Mrs Rogers. I tried to say no, but the only response was, "Oh come on there's no need for false modesty."

Twice already, I have completely forgotten to buy tickets. Luckily we wouldn't have won. I gave the money to charity; honestly, I did. I was too scared to own up and just to keep it would have felt like theft. I started buying eight weeks worth at a time so I didn't have to worry for a while. But then one week I couldn't remember if the tickets had been renewed or not so ended up getting them again when I didn't need to. That money came out of my own pocket, I could hardly ask for extra could I?

The worst ever though was the time I knew I had to renew the tickets but kept putting it off as it rained all week. I rushed out at the weekend in my usual panic arrived at the shop with minutes to spare and short one game card. The one with a single line was missing. Should I try racing home for it and risk not getting back to the shop? No better at least do the ones I did have but once I'd done that there'd be no time to return for the others. I think I could remember some of the numbers so I guessed the last line.

I watched the draw sat on the very edge of the sofa. My mouth was dry. As the dog tried to climb onto my lap, I irritably pushed him away. Instantly I regretted doing so, it wasn't his fault. I gave him a biscuit, bribing my way back into his affections. He ate it, then tentatively approached.

"No. Down, Rex, there's a good boy," I said.

I had eyes only for two lines of numbers. Those last six I guessed, and the ones I should have picked. The first number drawn was a two, not on either; the relief was enormous; at least it wouldn't be the big one. The second was thirty-seven; on both, that was one I did remember. Next thirty-eight; again on both, being consecutive is probably why I remembered them. Then twelve not on either, thank heaven. Then forty-one. What luck! Another on the list and amazingly one I had guessed correctly, could my luck hold out? Draw it quickly, I urged. I felt I couldn't breathe until they did and my brain has enough trouble functioning at the best of times. Oxygen starvation was not what I needed. No, no, no, forty-nine. It was on the game card but not the ticket I'd bought. Oh life was cruel. Four numbers! I should been ecstatic but my disorganisation meant we only had ten pounds between us when it should have been what... Hundreds? Thousands? I had no idea. Whatever it was we hadn't won it. What could I do? How could I explain at work?

Sunday was miserable. Not for Rex though, I knew I wouldn't sleep so I walked him for hours to try and tire myself out. As soon as I got to work, I blurted out the truth. I wanted people to know before they started thinking we'd won. It didn't make it all right of course but at least I could lessen the disappointment. Most people were understanding, sympathetic even. Not Sophie though, she tried to stir up trouble to make the others suspect I'd kept the money myself. Things were getting pretty tense until Mrs Rogers arrived.

"I checked the numbers myself and although this situation is disappointing I don't think Marie would have risked her job for £73 do you?"

Tempers cooled rapidly when people realised the sum involved was only about a fiver each.

"Perhaps we could get on with some work now? Marie a word please if you don't mind."

"So what exactly happened?" she asked once we were in her office. I told her everything. How I'd never wanted the task and how badly I'd carried it out. I knew I was hardly making myself look good but didn't know what else to do.

"Marie I believe that you just made a genuine mistake, now what shall we do about it?"

The 'we' reassured me it didn't look like I was about to get the sack at least. "I think I had better pay the winnings myself and persuade some one else take over the syndicate."

"Can you afford to pay?"

"Not without really cutting back for a while, but it would be worth it to get back the trust of the others and to not have the stress any longer."

"I'll pay it myself, but I have to say that I won't be able to offer you the office manager position, I don't think you're quite ready for the responsibility."

"I didn't know you were considering me. When you said at the meeting that you were considering two people I assumed you meant Sophie and Anne, I would have said something otherwise; the post wouldn't suit me at all."

"I am glad you can see that yourself. I was considering you because you are senior to both Anne and Sophie. Still let's get this all sorted out. Would you please ask Sophie to come and see me."

My heart sank. I could now understand why Sophie had been trying to cause me trouble. Surely, it would be worse now she was going to be my boss! I tried to concentrate on work until we were all called together for a meeting.

"First the lottery situation, I shall pay you myself and Marie will cease to run the syndicate."

"Yeah, get someone reliable to run it."

"Thank you, Sophie. I am sure we can all rely on you."

I tried not to smirk. She had manoeuvred herself into that as skilfully as she had done with me a few months earlier.

"As you know I will be cutting down my hours in preparation for retirement and have decided to appoint an office manager to take on some of my workload. I hope you will all give Anne your full support."

Everyone, with the exception of Sophie obviously, was pleased with the situation.

With Anne running things, life at work became almost a pleasure. That in itself would have been a happy ending, but things for me got even better the following weekend. You see when the lottery was handed over to Sophie, she said I'd chosen unlucky numbers and insisted we changed them. Everyone was furious with Sophie for making us change numbers the week before we would have won.

Once Sophie learnt what it felt like to be unpopular she stopped being unpleasant to me. Neither of us is rich now, but we are friends. I think that's far more important don't you?

6. Pursued To Glory

In the unexpected heat, Roger ran faster than he'd ever run before. Sweat poured from him, dripping into his eyes. It stung and blurred his vision but that didn't matter. In any case, he couldn't risk taking the time to glance behind to see if the men who chased him were close. If he paused, for even a second, they might catch him and then it would all be over for Roger and for Britain's hopes.

"If you and your men win on the land then you'll improve the moral of everyone else," his leader had told him. What failure would mean was left unsaid.

Roger wouldn't let down his countrymen, nor the women. Hadn't Churchill talked bravely about fighting on land, sea and air, even on the beaches? Roger would never surrender; he'd run until he could run no more.

His muscles ached and he was close to exhaustion. That didn't matter. It only mattered that he run faster than the men behind him, deliver what he carried to his countryman and that he do it before the Germans or the Japanese passed on their own burdens. That was vital.

Roger couldn't remember a time when he hadn't been able to run. Whilst other children took their first wobbly steps, Roger had raced confidently across the park.

"Ran rings around the other kids," his mum still told anyone who'd listen.

He'd not been gifted in other ways, but Roger could run.

At school, he'd been the fastest boy he knew. As he grew, he didn't lose that speed. That's why he'd ended up in his current position.

This wasn't his first battle, but it was the one that mattered. His earlier struggles seemed like little more than games compared with this last fight to earn his country a place on the world stage. His legs ached with the effort. Sweat soaked his clothes. Adrenaline pumped around his body. Roger took no notice. He ignored the screams around him, disregarded those whose sole aim was to cause him to fail. Roger simply did what he'd been trained to do.

He'd been recruited whilst still at school.

"You've got talent, lad," they said. "Fancy using it to help your country?"

What boy wouldn't? Roger attended a medical to ensure he was fit to serve his country and then started training. His job required strength, speed, courage and bravery. It took him away from his home and his family. He had success in small skirmishes to begin with and winning had seemed easy and inevitable. Later the fights had been harder and the rewards greater. When he'd returned home with a medal, those who knew him, and many who didn't, had been proud. The eyes of the nation and of the news reporters had been on him and his team then. Now he was under public scrutiny again. Every inch of ground won, every advance made, would be reported in the media. Every defeat too.

He was the third link in the process. At the start it had seemed the whole world was against him and his men, but soon he'd seen he needn't fear the Russians or the Americans. By the second stage, the French had been beaten and the Italians were overrun. His colleague had rushed at him and passed on the precious load without a word. Roger hadn't needed telling what to do. He ran. Every last reserve of his strength and concentration was focussed on safely reaching the man who could bring his side to victory.

Roger's heart pounded with the effort. Beside him, a Japanese man fell. Roger had no time for either pity or pleasure. The sound of a gunshot still seemed to ring in his ears, but Roger continued with his task. He ran. With what felt like his dying breath he thrust the precious object into the waiting hand of the Englishman in front of him. The man got away safely, leaving Roger alone, gasping for air. A second later, a German appeared at Roger's side. It no longer mattered; the man was no threat now. It appeared to Roger, that no country could beat Britain now.

He was right. With the contribution from Roger's relay team, Great Britain achieved a magnificent medal haul in the 2012 Olympic Games.

7. A Torturous Job

Igor loved his uniform. He kept it immaculately clean and neatly pressed. Pride and a sense of purpose filled him whenever he put it on. The severe black emphasised the strength in his lean body. In contrast, the innocent white of the tunic worn by his assistant, Tanya, emphasised her delicacy. After buttoning his jacket and combing his short hair, Igor studied his reflection. He nodded with approval; he was ready. For a moment, he considered delaying his departure. If he did so he'd arrive to find Tanya battling alone with the first agonised pleas of the day.

"I'm so pleased to see you, Igor," she'd whisper gratefully.

No; Tanya was one person who must never be tortured. He quickened his pace.

Igor loved his work. The sight of the squat, block-built building always made him smile. Swiping his security card to gain admittance filled him with a sense of belonging. His achievements granted him a fearsome reputation, but he didn't rely on it to gain respect; he didn't need to. He wasn't always fond of the people, but enjoyed the things he could do to them. He liked to think of them as clients and didn't care if they, or his colleagues, considered them as victims.

Igor loved his equipment; all of it. Well used and well maintained, it sparkled in fluorescent strip lighting, cast sinister shadows against stark white walls. Igor gazed at the racks of small, yet effective, items and wondered which he'd start with today. He patted one of the big frames used for stretching, almost as though it were a loyal pet. The machine would get some use today, so he checked each part was operating smoothly. He didn't want to miss words clients might utter, through clenched teeth, because of the irritating squeal of metal against metal. Igor picked up a length of rope, coiled it more neatly and placed it next to a simple wooden stick. Although he appreciated the traditional tools of his trade, Igor wouldn't be needing them today. Instead, he'd use something more high tech and cutting edge.

Igor loved the human body. Its complicated blend of resilience and vulnerability had always fascinated him. The incredible elasticity of a tendon never ceased to amaze him. When the body was forced into obedience with straps and bands, the muscles and sinews rarely resisted. He was honest; painfully honest. If he said 'this will hurt' then it did. He was careful never to push a client beyond their limits. He gave breaks for them to recover, so that they were able to fully participate in the next session.

Igor loved pain, sweat and fear; he preferred it when clients fought back. Igor always obtained good results, but the more difficult cases gave him the most satisfaction. A client who obeyed instructions without caring what happened to their bodies seemed a waste of his talents. Anyone could work with them and get the same result. Some of Igor's clients would never walk again. Some would try to wipe out all thoughts of him. Others would never forget him and the hours he spent working on their bodies. However hard the task, Igor always drew from each client everything their bodies had to give. Their minds were of less concern to him though of course he always acted as though interested in what they had to say; it was part of his job to listen.

Igor loved music; all kinds of music. He permitted his

clients the luxury of listening to whatever they wanted. Sometimes they doubted this offer, but they needn't for it was genuine. Even if he had to spend his own money and search in his own time, he would provide whatever music a client requested. If they expressed no preference he selected something from his own extensive collection. Often he felt that was the best option. It might be unwise for the individual to hear their favourite tune whilst Igor worked on them for they wouldn't like to remember the associations. Always, he let them choose.

Igor loved his assistant Tanya. The combination of strength and compassion she displayed astounded him. She'd whisper words of reassurance to those who awaited Igor's attentions and wipe away their tears. Gently she led them in to him and helped him with his work. Tanya brought them cool water when they begged for it. She smiled encouragingly, nodded sympathetically, but never permitted them to leave until Igor released them. Nothing scared Igor except the possibility that Tanya might reject his advances and shrink from him as so many others did. He never told her how he felt.

Igor loved and hated to stand before Tanya as she greeted him each morning. She smiled a welcome from her full lips and wide eyes. He took the day's schedule from her, careful not to allow his dark, muscular hand to linger against her pale, slender fingers.

"I'm so pleased to see you, Igor," she whispered and he allowed himself a second to hope.

"Mrs McCauley has scheduled an early appointment for her whiplash," Tanya explained.

He strode into the gym, fighting his disappointment. Igor loved his job as a physiotherapist, but it was torture to him.

8. What Friends Are For

Trying to push away my concerns, I returned the green dress to the hanger. It was the best yet, but that wasn't saying much.

The first one had been pink and frilly. Not my style at all, and that's not just because of my red hair. Even Chrissie looked doubtful when she'd asked me to try it on. I only agreed because this was for her special day and she's my best friend. You do stuff like for friends, don't you? Even if it involves the likes of Richard.

I'd believed he was another friend, but discovered my mistake last week. By then it was probably far too late. Would I speak out, or forever hold my peace? I didn't have long to decide.

Both Chrissie and the assistant had to stifle their giggles when I emerged from the changing room.

They weren't being mean, I knew the dress looked awful to the point of being comical. It somehow managed to make the parts of me it covered seem fat and dumpy and the exposed parts seem scrawny in comparison. I'm neither. I'm naturally tall and, thanks to all the exercise I'd been doing recently, trim and toned.

"No?" I said hopefully, after giving a twirl.

"No," Chrissie agreed.

The yellow wasn't frilly. On the right person it would probably have looked elegant, but that person wasn't me.

The skirt fitted so tightly over my thighs I felt trapped.

"One sudden movement and I'm going to split it," I said even before Chrissie got a proper look.

"That's no good then," she said.

"The green was fine colour-wise, fitted well enough and I could move in it," I said.

"It's not very bridesmaidy is it?" Chrissie said.

I agreed with her. If I'd had to wear a dress to work, instead of my usual suits, I'd have picked something like that. If this madness was to go ahead, then I might as well look the part. Richard of course was getting away with wearing a suit, so would be perfectly comfortable.

"Try the blue one," the assistant urged.

On the hanger it looked an unlikely bet. Too much bling and not enough of anything else, but I dutifully made the effort. It fitted fine. The top was surprisingly stretchy and once the silvery sequins were spread out a bit they looked less tacky and more, well, bridesmaidy. The skirt came down almost to my knees, but was kind of floaty and wrapped over at the front, so I was able to move easily.

"That's the one," Chrissie said the moment she saw it. "Really brings out the colour of your eyes and it shows off your legs. You've got great legs."

"Flattery will get you everywhere," I told her as I agreed I'd wear it. "Your turn now."

She tried on a huge white meringue, figure hugging satin number and something in cream lace. Chrissie is as slender and delicate as a pixie, with laughing eyes and cheeky grin to match. Everything looked good on her.

"This one I think, don't you?" she asked as she stepped out of the changing room in the lace outfit.

She seemed every inch the radiant bride looking forward to seeing her groom, and I really wished that wasn't the case. If you're thinking that's because I'm jealous, you'd be right.

"You look great," I assured her.

"Thanks. And thanks for doing this for me."

"What else are friends for?" I asked.

"Oh, let me see… they're the shoulder you cry on when you discover you have cancer. The hand you hold during chemo. The hug you need when your hair falls out."

"That's me. A useful collection of body parts! Some of them are hungry. I fancy pizza."

That last bit sort of worked. She did agree to share a meal with me and quickly changed back into her ordinary clothes as I paid the charity shop assistant for our dresses. They weren't expensive, but I knew that even those few pounds would go some way towards the research which might help prevent other people going through what Chrissie had endured.

Unfortunately I hadn't managed to get Chrissie to change the subject. She embarrassed me further by telling me again how she wouldn't have got through the last few years without me. How it was my loyalty and optimism, coupled with complete honesty which gave her hope when everything seemed impossible. The only time she paused was to give the waiter her order.

"Yeah, yeah, I'm a great friend. And I'm honest. That's why I've got to tell you… The thing is… Chrissie, you can't marry Richard."

There, I'd said it, even if I couldn't explain why. It's not Richard's fault he wasn't there for her through the chemo and stuff. He only joined the company, where we all work, after the worst was over. He and I became good mates, at least, that's how it seemed then.

Chrissie's surprised stare dissolved into laughter. "Of course I can't, Mike. Why on earth would you think I was going to?"

"He told me."

"You've obviously misunderstood. When he suggested the runaway bride theme for the sponsored run, I told him I'd like to be getting married for real, but not to him." She reached for my hand. "When it seemed my life was going to be cut short, I realised who I wanted to spend the rest of it with. You."

It wasn't Richard's words I'd misunderstood, but his motive. He really was my friend and had seen what I hadn't; I love Chrissie and she loves me. He'd persuaded us to dress for a wedding for the work's charity fun run. Then, when I failed to take the hint, had provoked my jealousy by claiming the sham wedding would become reality.

"Will you marry me?" I asked Chrissie, even though by then I knew the answer.

"Of course. In new outfits though, with less sequins on yours?"

"Definitely."

Tempting as it was to get Chrissie to beg Richard to be our bridesmaid and wear frilly pink, I'm going to ask him to be my best man. Isn't that what friends are for?

9. The Kidnap Of Petronella

What Molly really wanted was to learn to cope with her shyness. She'd never had a boyfriend; she was too shy to talk to anyone for long enough for them to ask her out. She knew it was holding her back at work too. Luckily for Molly she had a really supportive boss; Lydia.

"You have very good ideas, but because you're too self conscious to speak up in meetings, no one realises who made the suggestion. I know you work hard, but because you're quiet your achievements are easily missed by management."

Molly knew she was right, but didn't know what to do about it.

"I've reserved you a place on an assertiveness course. You don't have to go, but I hope you will."

"Assertiveness?" Molly asked, doubtfully.

"Yes, it's not about being aggressive or anything. It just helps you to cope with different situations. My brother used to be very shy; he went on this course, that's what gave me the idea."

"Did it stop him being shy?" Molly asked.

"Not completely, but he finds it easier to talk to people now. Are you happy to give it a go?"

Molly just nodded, she didn't have the nerve to contradict her supervisor's suggestion.

"After that, you might be better off in another department.

You could make a fresh start. You're good with figures; maybe you'd like to work in finance?"

Molly had occasionally been into the finance offices. It was always quiet there and most of the work was done on computers. There was also the attraction of Dishy Dave, the IT expert, whose office was located there. He'd never spoken to her, but his smile encouraged Molly to look forward to working within sight of him.

Her former colleagues surprised her with a card and gift. They'd all written nice things, saying she'd be missed and wishing her well. She didn't believe she'd be greatly missed, but was pleased they'd taken the trouble. Perhaps she'd been better liked than she realised.

The gift was a velvet kitten. Its fur was the exact same shade of pink as the sweater Molly often wore to work. The kitten wore a delicate silver chain with a shamrock and horseshoe.

"She's lucky," one girl told her.

"Put her on your desk and everything will go well in the new job," Lydia advised. "My brother's got one, except his is a dog. He says it helps."

"What will you call her?" they wanted to know.

"Petronella," Molly said, giving the first name that came to mind. Instantly she felt silly for saying something so fanciful.

"It suits her," the others decided.

"Best of luck, Molly. Don't forget to come back and let us know how you get on."

"Yeah and if you have any luck with Dishy Dave," they teased.

She didn't wonder how they knew she was attracted to

him. Every unattached girl in the company was pleased when her computer crashed; it meant he would soon be leaning over their keyboard. He was always polite, but never showed interest in any of them.

Molly was nervous attending the assertiveness course, so she took Petronella with her. Stroking the kitten's soft coat was enough to reassure her she was liked and that people wished her well. The course wasn't really so bad.

On her first day in the finance department, Molly stroked Petronella for luck, then walked in as confidently as she could. She remembered to smile as she'd been taught. Her new colleagues showed her to her new desk and introduced themselves. The department was much larger than she'd realised; Molly began to wonder if she'd made a mistake. That was until Dave arrived. Poor Molly was too self conscious to speak, but she smiled an acknowledgement of his greeting. Dave returned her smile.

The moment Molly placed Petronella on her desk the other girls began chatting to her. They asked where she'd got her and if she liked cats. Although Molly was very nervous, she remembered the advice from her course and was just about able to stay calm enough to answer their questions. She smiled at Petronella, the pink cat had helped her through the difficult morning. Petronella didn't return her smile, instead she slunk along behind the keyboard almost as if she might, at any moment, pounce on the computer mouse. The kitten was as successful at catching the mouse as Molly was at attracting the attention of Dishy Dave.

Each day it became easier for Molly to walk into her new office. She eventually managed to greet her colleagues without waiting for them to speak first. Once she even found the courage to say hello to Dave. He nodded at her before rushing off. Although a little disappointed that he'd not spoken to her, Molly felt proud that she'd spoken to him. She was still shy, but her nerves no longer stopped her from enjoying herself, nor were they a hindrance to her work. Molly hugged Petronella.

The kitten hadn't changed Molly. The course, her workmates and her own determination had all combined to do that, but Petronella was a symbol of her success. Maybe that's why Molly was so upset she was missing on Tuesday. Molly felt a stinging sensation in her eyes and heard sniggering behind her. Molly was reminded of the teasing she'd received at school and ran to the toilets.

She blew her nose and took a few deep breaths. This wasn't school, the girls she worked with weren't bullies and Molly was no longer the sort of person who hid in toilets. She returned to her desk.

On her diary was an envelope. Letters to spell her name had been cut from a newspaper and pasted on. Inside was a ransom note, demanding a packet of chocolate biscuits as the payoff. Molly laughed. Petronella's disappearance wasn't an unkind trick, it was a joke. Surely, that was a sign that she was liked? She wondered which of her new friends had done this, but although there were knowing smiles, no one admitted anything.

Later that morning Molly received another anonymous envelope. Inside was a photograph of Petronella surrounded by every single computer mouse in the office. At lunchtime, Molly bought the biscuits and shared them amongst the girls. Petronella was not returned. Instead Molly received an envelope containing some pink fluff. It wasn't the same shade as Petronella's fur, but the message was clear enough; the kidnapper did not consider Molly had met the demands.

An hour later another envelope arrived. The message stated she had one last chance to pay. She was to meet the kidnapper in The Red Lion after work.

The other girls read the note and laughed.

"Someone has gone to a lot of trouble to ask you out for a drink," was their opinion.

"Do you think so? Should I go?" Molly wondered why, if someone wanted to meet her, they didn't just say so.

"Yes, you must definitely go," she was told.

Molly had the distinct feeling she was the only person who didn't know what was going on. She did want Petronella back and was curious to see who had taken her; she'd have to go. She was pleased the meeting place was somewhere public, and that the bus home stopped outside.

Without Petronella, Molly was again feeling very shy as she walked into the pub, but she was able to overcome her nerves. She looked around the bar; there was no one she recognised. Molly didn't know what to do. She didn't want to buy herself a drink and sit alone, but she felt she couldn't leave just yet. Then she spotted Dishy Dave.

He must have heard about the kidnapping, everyone had been laughing about it all day. She'd ask him if she could sit with him, just until the kidnapper arrived.

She approached his table. Suddenly unable to explain, she instead held up the almost empty pack of biscuits in the hope that he'd guess, or at least speak first.

He did. "So, finally you've decided to pay up?"

"You're the kidnapper? But why?"

"It was my sister Lydia's idea. She knew my asking you out in the usual way might be awkward, you see we've got something in common." He stumbled over the words a little, leaving her in no doubt he meant they were both shy.

Molly dropped her gaze. For the first time, she noticed what was on the table in front of him. Petronella sat there, snuggled up to a blue, corduroy puppy.

"The girls in the office… they said, well they said… er, someone had gone to a lot of trouble to ask me out." She felt her face redden a much deeper shade than Petronella's fur.

"Yes. That was what … um."

Molly pulled out the chair opposite his and sank into it. "Yes, Dave. I'd love to have a drink with you."

10. The Mystery Postcard

Nancy Cahill filled her kettle and wondered why she'd bothered getting out of bed. In the two months since her retirement Nancy hadn't lost the habit of rising early. Now she was up it seemed sensible to make herself some breakfast. There was a whole day to get through before it would be time to sleep again. Perhaps later she might think of a pretext for calling on Margaret.

"Pop round anytime you fancy a chat," her former colleague had said.

"Thank you," Nancy had replied, but although she passed Margaret's home every week on her way into town, she'd never called without a specific invitation. She didn't want to be a nuisance.

She opened the fridge, dislodging a strawberry shaped magnet. Her mystery postcard slithered to the floor. She looked again at the image of palm trees silhouetted against a magnificent sunset. In the foreground was a table, topped with full cocktail glasses. The picture's message was clear enough; the sender was having a lovely time somewhere bright and exotic.

The card was addressed to Nurse Cahill at St Mark's. The school had kindly forwarded it. Nancy deciphered the untidy writing and read that the sender, Rebecca Sinclair, was thanking someone for making the trip possible.

"Rebecca Sinclair," Nancy said and shrugged. The name meant nothing.

When she'd received the postcard last week, Nancy considered taking it to Margaret. She'd been at St Mark's almost as long as Nancy and, as an ex-teacher, was more likely to remember pupils' names. Margaret probably received lots of lovely postcards, so wouldn't be interested in Nancy's single specimen. Besides, even if Margaret knew the girl, it wouldn't explain why Nancy had received the card.

She replaced the postcard next to a long white envelope, containing a concert ticket and held in place by a magnetic banana. Sipping her tea, Nancy thought about the concert ticket. Margaret had delivered it with a note suggesting they might travel together. Nancy loved violin music, so was almost tempted to go. She'd feel a fraud though, the ticket wasn't intended for a useless old nobody like her. The envelope also contained a photocopied letter from a former pupil of the St Mark's. He credited his success as a professional musician to the encouragement of his first music teacher, Margaret Wuthers. He'd given a generous quantity of tickets for a concert in his home town for, 'anyone who'd like to come, especially anyone who remembers me.'

"I do remember him, but I'm sure he won't remember his old school nurse," she'd told Margaret when they'd met at the supermarket one day.

"I expect he does, all the children seemed very fond of you," Margaret had said. Margaret always tried to be kind.

Of course, Nancy couldn't accept the ticket, but she could take it to Margaret today rather than waiting until she bumped into her in town as she'd planned. Margaret might invite her in for a cup of tea and perhaps help think of an explanation for the postcard.

Nancy's breakfast was almost ready when the post arrived. A letter had been forwarded by the school just like the postcard. The writing matched. She didn't open the envelope right away. It had been fun to guess how she'd received a postcard from Antigua by mistake; the letter would reveal the truth. With a mystery to solve and the possibility of a chat with Margaret to look forward to, Nancy enjoyed her breakfast.

She made herself a second cup of tea and opened the letter.

'Dear Nurse Cahill,

I don't suppose you remember me so that postcard I sent must of been a surprise. Sorry but what can I say? I'd been out in the sun all day and had a couple of cocktails before I sent it.'

Nancy smiled; she'd guessed correctly. It was good to know the sender had been enjoying herself.

'I'd better explain. I used to go St Marks. My name was Rebecca Verey then, but everyone called me Specky Becky.'

Oh yes, Nancy did remember her now. Margaret would too because the girl had helped behind the scenes at school concerts. She'd had no musical ability, but Margaret never excluded a child who wished to be involved and always found them something to do that made their parents proud. Margaret had been a real inspiration to all her pupils, not just the one who'd gone on to become a professional violinist. Maybe it was she the thanks were intended for?

'I wasn't any good at times tables and sometimes in tests, I'd tell Miss I wasn't feeling well and came to see you. I remember how you said it wasn't my fault if I wasn't clever, but it was my fault if I didn't do my best. After that I did try. The senior school gave me a good reference and said my

attendance was good so I got a job in a supermarket. 15 years later I'm still on the checkout, but it's not a bad job. I've got friends here and I get a discount on my shopping. I've done my best like you told me. I trained to be a first aider. It's not just because I get extra money. I thought it was a good thing to do and how you'd be proud of me.'

Nancy nodded. It was wonderful to hear of someone making the most of what she had and being happy with her lot. Even better was the knowledge that she'd played a small part in bringing this about.

'Anyway about the card. One day I was walking home from work when suddenly I found a man collapsed on the ground! He was having a heart attack and I was the only one there. I'm sure I saved his life (You must be proud of me now) He said I had anyway. He owns the travel agent near where we live. I didn't know that because we've never had the money to go in there. To thank me he gave us a holiday. I know it was a bit cheeky, but I said I'd always wanted to go somewhere with palm trees like that ad on the telly.

Mr Robyns (He's the man who had the heart attack) booked us on a trip to Antigua in the Caribbean. It was two weeks at one of those really fancy places where all the food and drink is free (which is how come I was drinking cocktails!!) Anyway that's why I sent the card because the holiday was to thank me and I wanted to thank you.

So thanks and I hope your well.

All the best.

Rebecca Sinclair (not Specky Becky anymore!)'

Well fancy that; Nancy had inspired this girl with the confidence to find a job she enjoyed and to go on to make a real difference in the world by saving a life. That was a real achievement. She'd given a version of that little pep talk to many other children who were struggling or lacking in confidence; perhaps she had made a difference to them too.

Nancy recalled a pep talk she'd once received from Margaret.

"Don't put yourself down, Nancy. Nursing is just as important as teaching. The children can't learn if they're ill or upset and you're very good at making sure they seldom are."

At the time, Nancy had thought Margaret simply wanted to make her feel better and was grateful for her kindness. Now she understood Margaret had really meant what she'd said. Maybe she'd also meant the offer to pop round anytime and the suggestion they occasionally go out together to visit places of interest or to share a meal. Nancy had thought Margaret's life was as full as hers was empty, but perhaps she was wrong about that too. How silly of her to have refused an offer of friendship. Luckily that was a mistake she could soon put right.

Nancy washed up quickly, put the card and envelope containing the ticket into her handbag and walked to Margaret's home.

"Come in, Nancy. It's so nice to see you."

"I wanted to discuss something with you, Margaret," Nancy said and removed the envelope containing the concert ticket from her bag.

"I hope you're not thinking of returning that? You love violin music and I'm sure Thomas's concert will be wonderful. I'm going to go."

"So am I. I wanted to ask if you'd like to meet up for a cocktail first?"

"I'd love too. Are we celebrating something?"

Nancy showed Margaret the mystery postcard and the letter.

"I inspired Rebecca just as you inspired Thomas, and I think it's only right that we celebrate the success of our former pupils."

"I couldn't agree more."

As Nancy walked home, she glanced into the travel agent's window. One of the posters showed palm trees silhouetted against a sunset, reminding her of her mysterious postcard. Nancy pushed open the door and stepped inside. A fortnight all inclusive in the Caribbean wasn't for her, but she might enjoy a coach trip to the West Country. Margaret might enjoy that too, so she'd collect a brochure for them to study. If Margaret didn't wish to accompany her, then Nancy would go alone and send her friend a postcard.

11. An Amazing Life

Dylis's watch had stopped so she wasn't sure if she was late for one bus or early for the next. A bit of both she decided as she was the only one there. With no commuters to watch and wonder about, she looked around her at the bus shelter. That didn't take long as it was just the standard roof over three plastic seats. The graffiti had been scoured away leaving a scratched smear, more unsightly than the words that were there before, and a vacancy the writer would no doubt feel obliged to fill on his next visit. The timetable was valueless without a watch to compare it to even if she'd been able to make out the tiny numbers through the blobs of gum. An absence of any external items of interest meant she'd have to use her memories for entertainment. She chuckled to herself as she idly wondered which part of her amazing life she should try to recall.

A pigeon on a high wall to her left was making a fuss. Dylis wondered what it was attempting to communicate and how long it had been there before she'd noticed it. The bird wasn't hoping for a reaction from her, she knew, but still she felt guilty for having ignored it. The pigeon dropped down to the row of advertising hoardings, sidling along a metal rail until it disappeared behind a poster promoting low calorie chocolate. Of course the bird couldn't read, but as it emerged its ruffled feathers and apparently mocking cry seemed to correspond with her own opinion of such a concept.

He, Dylis supposed the pigeon was a he, took a few more sideways steps toward a reminder to passers-by that their tax returns were imminently due. The noise level increased sharply as another pigeon's head emerged from behind the board. Her pigeon screamed and stamped its feet as the second pigeon was joined by a third and a fourth. They made a terrific racket as they lunged at the first bird. Three onto one wasn't fair; why didn't he fly away? They were going for his head. Her pigeon seemed to be choking as one of the others held its open beak… Wait a moment, the weren't fighting. She'd seen something like this on a television wildlife programme. Her pigeon was regurgitating food into the mouths of her offspring. As far as she could recall, male birds could do it too, but now she'd seen it bringing food to its young, it looked to Dylis like a female. Was it wrong of her to have changed her mind about the bird's sex like that, or just a symptom of her age?

Baby pigeons! Dylis had thought nobody ever saw them. These weren't exactly babies, but certainly youngsters. Now she looked carefully she could see that. How lucky she was to have had the chance to see them feeding. If it hadn't been for chatting to Sharon, she'd have been out the shop earlier and caught the bus straight away and missed it. The chicks must have been there for weeks, hatching and growing without her being aware of their presence. Then on the very day that Sharon told her she'd lived an amazing life, Dylis saw them.

Sharon was a young woman who'd recently begun volunteering in the same charity shop at which Dylis worked every Wednesday and Saturday. Today had been the first time the two women had spent much time together and they'd chatted away comparing their various lifestyles. Dylis thought Sharon's life was rather amazing; amazingly hard work. She was a single mother of three children, one of whom was disabled. She cared for them with almost no family support and even less money. Now they were all at school, Sharon was hoping to get a job to improve their financial position.

"That's why I'm working in the charity shop, to get used to the routine and hopefully get a good reference."

"Very sensible," Dylis said. Everything about Sharon seemed so sensible it was difficult for Dylis to see how the younger woman had got herself into the difficult position of having three children but no husband to support them.

Still things were different now from when Dylis grew up. She hadn't even kissed a boy until she was sixteen – the age at which Sharon had first fallen pregnant. The boy, Dylis's, not Sharon's, had been the son of the neighbours. At eighteen, Walter had seemed sophisticated with his quiffed hair, leather jacket and winkle picker boots.

Sharon had found all this fascinating. "Did you go jiving?"

Dylis laughed. "I did, although my poor mother couldn't understand what was wrong with a nice waltz."

Dylis had been seventeen before Mother would allow her to go with Walter to the pictures or dancing at The Victory Hall without her older sister as chaperone. Walter had proposed when Dylis was eighteen. Mother and Father had allowed her to wear his ring around her neck, but wouldn't allow them to even consider setting a date for the wedding until Walter had completed his apprenticeship. They, and Dylis's friends, had cautioned her against rushing into anything.

Sharon had expressed surprise that Dylis hadn't resented what the younger woman saw as a restrictive upbringing.

"Oh no, Sharon. I admit I did spend the occasional afternoon drinking frothy milkshakes with Walter when Mother thought I was at the library with friends, but I knew they were just concerned for me and didn't want me to make a mistake I'd later regret."

"Like getting pregnant by a bloke with no job who'd clear off before the baby was born?"

"Yes. Not being able to marry Walter… Oh, my dear is that what happened to you? I'm sorry, I didn't think."

"Don't worry. I made mistakes, but I love the kids and wouldn't change a thing."

Dylis had nodded to indicate agreement. Sharon's face had glowed with pride as she'd shown Dylis the pictures of her children. They'd looked clean and happy. Dylis was sure they were greatly loved.

She looked now at her pigeon as it sidled out, peaceful at last. It hopped back to the top of the wall, stretched its wings and flew away. Feeding that brood had to be a struggle and the bird seemed to be alone, but raw instinct ensured it would repeat this cycle several times. The bird couldn't change that.

Would Dylis change her life if she could? What would have happened if she'd defied her parents' wishes and married Walter when he'd asked? Bit late to start thinking about that now. She'd married when she was twenty-two and like Sharon, had three children whom she loved very much. Dylis decided that, just like Sharon, she wouldn't change a thing. She didn't even regret missing the bus.

Dylis smiled and allowed her mind to drift to the moment she'd first realised she was pregnant, to the memory of her three children bringing her breakfast in bed on Mother's Day, the first time she'd held her granddaughters. Back and forth she went in time to when she'd seen The Beatles live and watched her family sing happy birthday via Skype because she'd been away on holiday. That holiday, seeing Sri Lanka so long after dreaming in Geography lessons of a trip to Ceylon. Walter on his moped coming to collect her for a dance, passing her driving test. So many happy memories.

Loud squawking brought her back to the present. The pigeon had returned. Now she knew what was happening, those cries held a hint of maternal urgency. Dylis watched carefully so that she could tell Sharon all about it. Dylis was sure her new friend would also find the experience amazing. Dylis wouldn't have to rely on just telling Sharon, she could show her. Maybe they'd be very lucky and the baby pigeons would still be there the following Wednesday. She couldn't count on it though, they looked almost as large as their mother. Dylis would be coming out again tomorrow to visit the caterers who were providing the food at her golden wedding celebration. She'd ask Walter to bring his camera and photograph the chicks. He'd been with her for all of her amazing life, she wasn't about to allow that to change.

12. Offside Rule

I didn't think much of Aaron when I first saw him. His family moved next door just before Christmas. We looked out the windows to see what they were like. There was a lady and man and a boy. He had glasses and walked funny. He didn't help carry stuff, but the way he acted when a computer was unloaded, you could tell it was his. There was no bike.

When the furniture lorry left, Mum went round to see if they'd like a cup of tea. They all came. Mum gave us cake too, even though it wasn't tea time. Mum and the lady chatted, the man didn't say much, and Aaron didn't speak at all. Mum invited them to come round for supper. Don't know why, we don't have supper.

"That's very kind, but we're just going to have a takeaway and an early night. It's been a busy couple of days."

The next day Mum said I should invite Aaron round to play. I think she felt sorry for me because none of my school friends live near, so I'm sometimes a bit lonely in the holidays. I didn't think he looked much fun but I didn't have anything better to do. He came. Mum gave us juice and biscuits. I couldn't think what to say, just asked him about his school. He'd left and was coming to mine after the holiday. Mum said we could watch a video. Then we played draughts for a bit. He was pretty good at that and beat me three games to two. Then he went home.

Next day I was invited round there. He showed me his

electronic games. We had a few goes then looked up loads of stuff on his computer. Aaron showed me the website for Portsmouth Football Club. That was cool; Aaron's a Pompey fan too. There was a thing where we looked at the earth then zoomed in on towns. He typed in Portsmouth, England and found our road. Then we looked at Australia where my gran and granddad live. I nipped back home to ask mum for their address.

"You're back quick. I hoped you'd be his friend."

"I'm going back and his mum said to ask if I can stay for tea."

"You're a good boy, Michael."

I thought she was going to kiss me so I went back to Aaron's sharpish.

I stayed with Aaron all evening. I couldn't think why I hadn't liked him before.

For Christmas, I got a new bike. I thought I'd better ask Aaron if he wanted a go on it.

"I can't ride a bike, Michael."

"I'll teach you if you like."

"No, it's because of my leg. It doesn't work right, it's been like that since I was born."

He showed me scars from some operations. Now I knew why he walked funny and his mum drove us to the pictures instead of getting us to walk.

"Does it hurt?"

"Nope, I have injections so it doesn't."

When term started Aaron's mum took him in the car. She took me too, when it rained, otherwise I went on my new bike. It rained a lot so we had most break times indoors.

Aaron brought some of his best games and he let all my mates play with them. He told them jokes and always knew lots of amazing stuff. Teachers liked him too. He was much cleverer than me, but didn't go on about it like some of the girls do.

Things were fine until after half term. We were all pleased that we were allowed to use the football pitch again. The caretaker wouldn't let us before, he said it was flooded. It wasn't really, just pretty muddy, but the teachers said we couldn't use it. We played a lot, to make up for when we couldn't. Aaron didn't play.

"Wouldn't be much good would I?

I thought he was just sulking because he didn't like football and it was something I could do better than him. It's the taking part that matters not the winning, my dad says. I would have told him that, but he went off on his own.

I didn't go round his house for a couple of days. Now I had my bike I could meet my friends down the park. We played football until it got dark. One day I managed a fantastic sliding tackle. Everyone was well impressed so I did an action replay. Big mistake. I broke my leg. It hurt.

I was taken away in an ambulance. Shame I was hurting too much to really notice. Another time I would have enjoyed that. I had a cast put on and Mum and Dad took me home. They made a fuss of me; allowing me pizza and coke. Aaron came round and brought his games. He talked to me for ages and lent me the dragon chasing game. He's a good mate.

After a few days, I went back to school. Aaron's mum took us both. I had crutches and the teachers were really nice. At lunchtime, the others wanted to play football.

"That's not fair, I can't run."

"You can still play if you want. We don't mind if you're rubbish."

"Don't be daft. If I tried to kick a ball I'd fall over."

I went off to look for Aaron. He moved his bag so I could sit next to him on the bench. "All right, mate?"

I said I was, but it wasn't true. I didn't like being left out. I stared at my leg, Aaron's foot was next to mine, stuck out in that funny way it always does. I thought I could guess why he didn't like football.

"Aaron, if you kicked a ball would you fall over?"

"Yes."

I thought for a bit. It wasn't fair we couldn't play. I'm ace at football and Aaron's really smart. We should be able to join in.

"Managers."

"Eh?"

"We can be football managers. I'll be Harry Redknapp, you can be Luiz Felipe Scolari."

"I don't want to be Scolari. He talks funny."

"Yeah well, so do you."

"Do not."

"Do too."

"Race you to the touchline."

Aaron beat me. I didn't really mind, I guessed he didn't win many races. I did mind when his team beat mine every lunch break. It was better at the weekends. His mum drove us to the park. He was manager and I was coach. We won nearly every game. When I could play again we kept Aaron on as manager. We kept winning. I was pleased about the winning, but I think Aaron just liked taking part.

13. A Bad Habit

Orange spray paint informed anyone who was interested that, 'Tezzer waz ear'. Maureen's only interest was to wonder if the paint on the seat in the bus shelter was dry enough for her to sit and complete a sudoku puzzle as she waited for the ever late number 39 into town. It probably was; the graffiti was much more likely to have been sprayed one evening over the weekend than early on Monday morning. She had to be sure though; unlike the youths who regularly hung around there in ripped jeans and matted hair, she took pride in her appearance and wouldn't want to ruin her clothes.

She opened her handbag to look for a tissue. There was only one and she might need that. Maybe she could find a dropped bus ticket or other piece of relatively clean paper among the rubbish at her feet that would suffice to test the paint. Maureen nudged the rubbish with the toe of her shoe. As she'd feared, nestling amongst cigarette buts and crisp packets was a broken beer bottle and a syringe. Disgusting!

She never walked along this street at night; she wouldn't feel safe. Maureen couldn't pick up the litter without risk to her health; not that she should have to clear up after the youths who congregated here in the evenings vandalising the bus shelter and disturbing local residents. These hooligans, especially the drug addicts, should be locked up; they were liars and thieves with no consideration for anyone else. There was no excuse for their actions, as she often tried to explain to Shona, her friend at work. Shona always tried to make excuses for them.

"It's not always their fault. They have difficult home lives, some of them, and aren't always set good examples."

Maureen could well believe the teenagers didn't know any better. They seemed very poorly educated. If her own spelling and grammar were as poor as theirs, she'd try to keep the fact private until she learnt to improve, not advertise it with fluorescent graffiti on public surfaces. If they felt their remarks worthy of being written down, why not do so in proper English? Maureen always had a pen in her bag and she itched to correct the graffiti to, 'Terry was here' and possibly add 'but would have been better off at school learning to write.' She could do it; the seat was already ruined. Somebody should teach these youths something. Maybe she'd better not. If they guessed it were her, they might retaliate in some way. Not that they needed a reason. At any moment one of them could appear and attempt to intimidate her just for being in the wrong place at the wrong time.

"Good morning, Maureen."

The familiar sight of Duncan, the local beat bobby and Shona's husband, as he passed on his bicycle, should have reassured her, but it seemed the police weren't interested in dealing with drug related crime. They should act decisively, especially when the offenders were young. 'Nip it in the bud', she wanted to tell them. They wouldn't take any notice of her though. Maureen often reported the youths who hung around outside her home to Duncan.

"I've just seen them handing something round. You should get down here right now and search them all," she said when she called.

"Can't you confiscate their money, so they can't buy drink

and drugs?" she'd suggested to Duncan. "Or have them followed so they can't go and buy them."

She was wasting her breath; nothing was ever done. Instead she simply nodded at Duncan from her seat inside the bus shelter.

The bus was late as usual. Maureen supposed the college students were to blame for that; there were so many of them and they always messed about as they boarded or left the bus. She eventually retrieved her pass from her bag and flashed it at the driver before looking around for a seat. An untidy boy was very offhand as he offered her his seat and another had the cheek to call her 'love' as he handed Maureen the purse he'd snatched at the moment she dropped it. Teenagers were so rude.

Even at work, she didn't feel safe. Youths could try to break in and steal things to feed their habits.

"Morning, Maureen," Shona called as she walked in. "Coffee?"

"Please," Maureen said and opened her newspaper at the crossword.

"Thanks, Shona. Did you have a good weekend?" Maureen asked when a steaming mug was placed on her desk.

"Yes, not bad. You?"

"Except for the yobs keeping me awake all night."

"You'll be glad to know my hubby is doing something to tackle the problem."

"Excellent."

"It's a great idea. He's setting up a kind of youth club. It'll keep them off the streets and away from drink and drugs for a while. Duncan is hoping to get them interested in more worthwhile pastimes. Sport for example."

Maureen snorted, but that didn't stop the flow of enthusiasm from Shona.

"He'll give advice about drugs and involve members of the community. He thinks if the kids know people, they'll be less likely to target them for muggings and the like. He's hoping you'll agree to help."

"Me? Why would I want to help a bunch of druggies?"

"It's more to help prevent them becoming drug addicts. It seems most of them first experiment with drugs out of boredom."

"Maybe, but I'm sometimes bored. Instead of turning to drugs, I find something to occupy me. Besides, I don't see why it's my responsibility."

"This is to help make your area safe. You've been moaning for months that something should be done."

"You're right, I have. I do think it's a good idea to catch these kids before they start causing problems and your husband is to be commended, but even if I wanted to, I don't see how I could help. It's not as though I have any experience of these matters."

That was a cheap shot, Maureen admitted, but she didn't like being lectured on her duty. She knew Shona's brother had recently been arrested for possession of cannabis, to the embarrassment of her husband.

"I think you'd be great. You'd be able to sympathise as you've got your own addiction," Shona snapped.

"If you're talking about my smoking, that's not the same at all."

"Really?" Shona switched on her computer as though the conversation was ended.

"Yes! I didn't understand the risks when I started and I've not smoked one for more than three weeks and the one I had then was just a tiny lapse. I still go to the support group and use the patches and gum, but I …" She trailed off, Shona would probably just point out druggies didn't understand the risks and needed help and support too.

"See, you'd be great at showing the kids that it's possible to give up bad habits and, as you've been on Television, they'd have respect for you."

Maureen sat up straight. There had been a great deal of fuss over her appearances on Countdown during her six week run, but people had mostly stopped talking about it now. "Do you think they'd have seen me?"

"Oh yes. The programme is a bit of a cult amongst teenagers, especially students and those who've just left school and haven't yet got a job. The people Duncan's trying to help are in that age group. You were a very popular contestant too."

"That's true."

"Tell you what, we'll make it a challenge. If you give up your addiction for two weeks, I promise not to nag you about smoking or anything else ever again. If you can't quit, you promise to stop moaning about the teenagers and try to help them instead."

"Fine," Maureen agreed.

"But, I reckon you're going to have to admit you share a problem with the kids who get into drugs."

Of course she didn't.

"Shona, I have only had three cigarettes in the last three months. I can go two weeks without one."

"I know you can, you're doing brilliantly! Giving up

crosswords and puzzles is going to be much tougher for you." Shona closed Maureen's paper.

By the end of the working day, Maureen did feel a little irritable, but that was just because she got so bored at lunchtime. At home, she finished the crossword from the paper and did three from her puzzle book. Well, she'd already answered a few clues that morning, so a few more in the evening weren't going to make any difference.

On Tuesday, Maureen announced she needed to go to the bank in her lunch break. She sat in the park and completed the newspaper crossword. Just one isn't an addiction, is it?

After lunch, Shona glanced at Maureen's newsprint stained fingers. "You've been puzzling."

Maureen shook her head.

"If you're not doing the crosswords, you won't need your paper, puzzle book and pen. Hand them over."

Maureen did so. She didn't offer to make Shona a coffee when she next stopped for a break.

On Wednesday morning, Shona insisted on checking Maureen's bag and confiscated the new puzzle book and spare pen she found. Maureen tried to borrow the crossword page from a colleague when Shona went to lunch, but everyone refused. They wouldn't believe her assertions that the agreement had been just for a few days, just to cut down.

On Thursday, Maureen saw a newspaper in someone's bag and helped herself. She needed a pen and began a frantic search. Someone came in before she'd found one and Maureen was forced to make a hasty exit to the lavatory.

The lady who'd almost caught her rifling through the handbags offered Maureen a lift home. "It's filthy weather out there. You won't want to stand at the bus stop."

Indeed Maureen didn't. She accepted the lift with gratitude and guilt. "I don't want to put you to any trouble."

"No trouble at all. I don't live far from you. Actually I could give you a lift most days. It'd be nice to have company on the drive."

"I didn't know you'd moved."

"I haven't. Oh… I did say it wasn't convenient for me to go down your road, I remember now. Sorry about that, but it was just because you smoked in my car the one time I did give you a lift. I have asthma …"

"I'm sorry. I hadn't realised."

Maybe that's what Shona had meant about Maureen having a bad habit in common with the drug users. She had at times been inconsiderate of others by smoking in their presence. She was unsociable with her crosswords too. She didn't speak to people at lunchtimes and took up more than her fair share of space in the canteen by spreading out her paper.

Because Maureen had accepted a lift, she didn't pass the shop to buy another puzzle book on her way home. She later went out in the dark, past the bus stop where troublesome youths often lurked, to buy one.

The girl who held the door open for Maureen wore a huge jacket that was probably stuffed with things she'd stolen. On her way back, Maureen saw a group of hoodied youths approaching. She rushed home with a pounding heart and dry mouth.

Once safely inside, Maureen caught sight of her desperate expression in the hallway mirror. Three days ago, she'd promised a friend she'd stop puzzling. Since then she'd lied, stolen and taken a risk with her own safety. She'd put a friendship and her job at risk all to get her puzzle fix. She was as bad as any other addict.

Once she'd completed a suduko grid, just to calm down, Maureen made a phone call. Duncan seemed delighted with her offer of assistance for his youth club project.

"Shona said you needed time to think about it."

"Tell Shona she's only nearly always right."

14. Buying Bread

Wilbur Green stood back to allow the woman in the suit to order her sandwich ahead of him. He wasn't in a hurry; it always took him a long time to decide. On offer was bread, brown, granary, wholemeal or white in slices, or rolls or baguettes in the same options. If he didn't fancy that he could plump for a wrap, panini or wheat free rice cakes. The choice of fillings was even wider and then he had to select sauces, salad items and seasoning.

"Hiya, Wilbur," the pretty little assistant greeted him. "We've got a special offer on today. Would you like that?"

"Yes please, my dear."

Wilbur took the hot meatball sandwiches back home to his wife, trying not to worry what he'd do once the shop closed down. There'd always been a shop on the corner of his street. When he was a kid it had been a sweet shop. Later it was the newsagent's which gave him his first job. Then it had been the craft shop where Edith had worked. Without that shop maybe he'd never have had a wife and child?

For a short time there had been a fancy little bakery there. The delicious smell of baking bread had reached him every morning as he got up for work. He used to run down there, before he'd even had a cup of tea, and buy a warm loaf or a couple of rolls to eat with his wife.

By the time their Emma arrived the corner shop was a convenience store. It had been so useful to nip down there for the things they needed. Wilbur had noticed it being used less and less over the years. Most people used the big out of town supermarkets where there was more choice and lower prices.

Wilbur didn't think more choice was such a good thing. When all he wanted was a loaf he was confronted with a bewildering array of bread products. Last time Emma took them to the supermarket he'd attempted to count the whole range. At thirty-seven he was still on the first side of the first aisle.

It was good of Emma to come and take them shopping, but Wilbur would much rather there was a corner shop he could pop to for his and Edith's daily needs and that those big supermarkets had never forced all the small, local shops out of business.

Edith looked up from her lunch. "You all right?"

He smiled. "Fine, my love."

"No you're not, Wilbur Green!"

Dear Edith. She might not be able to walk more than a few steps but her mind was as sharp as ever. He was lucky in that. Wilbur told her about the sandwich shop closing down.

"What are you going to do about it?" Edith asked.

"Do? I can't do anything."

"Course you can. You always put things right."

Maybe he should protest? He didn't have all that much else to do and there was just a chance someone would take notice.

Every morning after breakfast, Wilbur wheeled Edith down to the shop. They held a placard saying, 'save our shop' which the staff had helped make.

"If it works you'll save our jobs," they'd said.

Wilbur and Edith rather enjoyed their protest. People often stopped to chat. Many remembered the previous convenience store or wished there was one there now. It wasn't just people Wilbur's age who said they'd like one. Young mums would appreciate such a store too, as taking small children into the huge supermarkets was rarely a pleasant experience. Those who had the time to spare would often stop to join in the protesting.

It must have been a slow news time because both the local paper and radio station came to talk to Wilbur and Edith. They invited listeners and readers to write or call in with memories of previous shops on that corner and suggestions of what they'd like instead. It seemed every single one of them agreed with Wilbur. Even a spokesman from the big supermarket replied with some rot about them sympathising with those who missed traditional small shops and claiming that, despite them being a countrywide company, they still wanted to serve the local community.

Sadly though it was all to no avail. The closing day come with no news of a reprieve.

As well as the newspaper and radio reporters, a man from the local TV news arrived. He asked if they could film Wilbur.

"Film me doing what?" Wilbur asked.

"Answering questions about your protest, just as you've done on the radio."

Wilbur shrugged. "Bit late to do any good now, but I don't mind."

He was interviewed and felt better after he'd had his moan about the big supermarkets and explained how, what the reporters referred to as 'vulnerable people', were those most in need of a local shop selling the basic necessities at a reasonable price. The reporter took Wilbur's phone number so he could let him know when the piece would be on.

The television reporter called again a few days later; to invite Wilbur and Edith to the studio. The reporter drove them both in and was kind to them. He fetched them tea and introduced them to the anchorwoman who was just as charming in real life as she appeared on the TV. Wilbur and Edith were settled on the sofa along with a man Wilbur didn't recognise.

The anchorwoman introduced them all to the viewing public. The stranger was revealed to be a spokesperson for the area's biggest supermarket chain. Wilbur geared up to give the man a piece of his mind, but the younger man cut him off.

"Mr Green," he said. "I have what I think will be good news for you. The shop on the corner of your road has been acquired by my company."

"That's really rubbing salt into the wound! Your company drives all the little shops out of business and now you're buying up the only chance of anyone competing with you. Don't you ever stop to think of anything other than profits?"

The man listened with exaggerated patience before saying, "We do want to serve the local community which is why we'll be opening a small branch in the now empty building which was formerly your local sandwich shop."

"Oh." It wasn't much of a reaction, but Wilbur wasn't sure how he felt. He wasn't convinced the supermarket people were doing it out of the goodness of their hearts, but almost anything was better than a boarded up store.

Edith wasn't in any doubt. She squeezed his hand and whispered, "You did it, Wilbur. You got our shop back."

"Of course we won't be able to offer our full range," the supermarket spokesman continued. "But we'll stock all those basic items you're likely to need."

"Suits me," Wilbur grudgingly admitted.

"I'm glad you approve."

Wilbur couldn't help answering the man's smile. Poor chap was only doing his job and, even though it was owned by a big supermarket chain, having a proper shop on the corner would make Wilbur and Edith's lives much easier.

"We were hoping you might open it, Mr Green."

"Me?"

"Yes, you've become a bit of a local celebrity."

"Have I now? Well maybe I can use what little clout that brings to get jobs for the girls from the sandwich shop?"

"I promise that if they wish to apply, their applications will be given full consideration."

Wilbur hadn't felt anything like a celebrity before, but he was treated like one for weeks afterwards. Whenever he took Edith out for a breath of air people stopped them to say they'd seen him on television and how pleased they were that they'd soon have a proper corner shop.

One of these said, "You don't know me, Mr Green but my daughter used to serve you in the sandwich shop. Jenny Rice?"

"Lovely girl," Wilbur said. He wasn't entirely sure which one was Jenny, but as they were both lovely it didn't matter.

"Thanks to you, she and her friend got job interviews for the new store. They haven't heard yet, but we're hopeful they'll both be taken on."

"That's good news. Please give Jenny and… her friend my

best wishes."

At nine o'clock sharp on the opening day for the new shop, Wilbur cut the ribbon and Edith accepted a store gift voucher.

She opened the envelope and peeped inside. "That'll keep us in fresh bread and more for a good while, Wilbur."

Wilbur brushed aside the thanks of the sandwich shop girls in their supermarket uniforms, saying, "It was pure selfishness, I just wanted to keep seeing your lovely smiles."

He headed off to see how many types of bread his new shop had on offer. If they had any of those fancy things with chocolate he might just try them for elevenses. Or perhaps they'd have a nice crusty bloomer, or crumpets.

"You're going to have to chose, Edith. If you leave it to me, I won't have made a decision in time to have whatever it is with our morning coffee."

15. The Spirit Of Christmas Present

Vicki dashed to the toilet. Her hasty exit was nothing to do with the reduced-price seafood salad she'd had for lunch. Vicki had seen a colleague approach with a sponsorship form. The woman had told everyone how she planned to run ten miles to raise money for some African child's eye operation. Charity should begin at home, that was Vicki's motto.

When she returned to the office, Vicki's colleague, Philippa, asked if she felt ill. Philippa was the only one to show concern; the rest of their colleagues were discussing the Christmas party.

"I'd like to suggest a change this year," Lisa said. "Instead of giving cards to everyone and getting several presents, why don't we just get one gift that's really good?"

"I was going to ask what you usually do about cards and presents," Sandra, the new girl, said.

"Up to now we've bought cards for everyone, personally I think that's a bit wasteful. We all put our names on three bits of paper, put them in a hat and draw three out to decide who we buy gifts for. They're wrapped and tags with the recipients name are added, but who bought them is secret," Lisa explained.

"That sounds like fun," Sandra said.

"And during the last week we bring in cakes and chocolates and stuff. Mind you most of us shouldn't be eating them," Philippa added.

Vicki didn't know if she wanted a change. She liked all the free goodies that were brought in. There was so much, she'd never needed to contribute anything. She agreed that buying all the cards was a waste, Christmas had become far too commercial; although she admitted, the cards she received did bring a bit of cheer to her flat. She didn't bother with decorations. Why spend out on something you only see for a few weeks a year?

A really good present would be nice though. Vicki didn't get given many presents. There was always something practical from her son, it never occurred to him to buy her anything luxurious or frivolous. She'd hinted a few times.

"Not really your style is it, Mother?" was his only comment.

The girls from work didn't usually choose anything practical. Over the years, she'd received some lovely gifts. The suggested limit was five pounds, but some people clearly spent much more. Vicki never exceeded five pounds. In fact, in six years of buying three gifts she'd not yet reached a total outlay of that amount.

The first year she was given a set of four beautifully painted cups and saucers. Vicki had no need of them, her mugs were fine. She had wrapped them separately, in secondhand paper, thus providing one present for the next four years. Once she was given a selection of toiletries in a little basket. Those too had been split meaning she'd not had to buy anything at all the following year. The basket was refilled with the free samples that were regularly pushed through her letterbox, and decorated with ribbons saved from the flowers Philippa had given for her birthday. Twice Vicki had been given books, she read them, but was careful to have clean hands and not leave marks, so she could use them as gifts. Charity shops were a good source of ornaments. Occasionally they sold old stock for just a few pence.

Vicki saved wrapping paper from the previous year or collected the sheets that supermarkets provided for wrapping flowers. Old greetings cards were recycled as gift tags.

Lisa offered to ask around and see what everyone thought about the proposed new arrangements. Vicki was concerned that if only one gift was to be given she would have trouble finding something suitable at a price she was prepared to pay, but diplomatically declared herself happy to go along with the majority.

Later that week a girl from dispatch came round shaking an envelope.

"I'm collecting for a party and games for deprived inner-city kids."

Vicki thought it was up to the families to provide for them. How deprived could they be in a welfare state? Vicki had long ago vowed she would never again allow herself to be caught out by a charity scam. As though it hadn't been thirty years ago, Vicki remembered the sick, hollow feeling when she'd discovered the truth about the money she'd given her former friend. It had not been for urgently needed medical treatment that could only be obtained abroad. Instead the woman had taken Vicki's carefully saved house deposit and gone on a spending spree. After years of scrimping and saving, Vicki eventually managed to buy a home, but she still hadn't regained her trust or generous spirit.

She couldn't avoid the girl who'd approached her desk, seeking donations, so reached into her bag and dropped some coins into the envelope. Vicki kept a supply of pennies, plus any foreign coins, washers and shiny buttons she came across, ready for this type of situation.

"Thanks, Vicki. Have you heard about the Christmas arrangements?"

"I heard there might be a change."

"Yes, we're just going to buy one present. No one's to go over fifteen quid though. Management decided."

"Don't worry, I'm sure Vicki won't be breaking that rule," Philippa said.

Vicki had just ten days to find a gift. She had drawn Philippa. That had never happened before. Philippa was the closest she had to a friend. Vicki had to get her something nice, but what? She walked around the shops, looking for suitable presents. She did buy a half-price sweater that would suit her son perfectly, but there was still Philippa's gift to find. The charity shops didn't have sales at Christmas. There was a pretty crystal vase, but that cost seven pounds; too much to pay for a piece of secondhand glass. In desperation, Vicki even looked through the cupboards in her flat, but there was nothing suitable she wished to part with.

The following morning's mail provided the answer. She had filled out a form some time ago, that promised three free-trial romantic novels, plus a charming pendant for replying promptly. The books were no good; she wouldn't have time to read them before they were wrapped. The pendant however, did have possibilities. Vicki had recently bought herself a new skirt which had ribbons sewn into the waistband for hanging. She cut one off and threaded the pendant onto it. Now she needed a box. The plastic pouch it had come in declared it to be a free gift and so must be discarded. With time running short, she realised she would have to buy one. The cheapest she could find was rather big and even that cost almost a pound. Luckily, Vicki had some cotton wool she'd saved from the tops of Milk of Magnesia bottles. She could use that as packing and it would smell nice and fresh too.

On the final work day of the year, Vicki added her contribution to the pile. She looked, but couldn't see which was hers. After lunch, the staff gathered and the gifts were given out. She recognised the wrapping paper as the pendant was lifted from the pile.

"Oh dear, the tag is missing," Lisa said. "We'll leave it to last and see who doesn't have one."

Soon another package with a missing label was found. The gifts were given out, until only Philippa and Vicki had been given nothing.

"Well there are two left, who wants which?" Lisa asked.

"You chose," said Philippa. "I'm sure that both of them will be lovely."

One had the second hand paper Vicki had used last night to wrap the cheap pendant; the other was much larger, in metallic paper and trimmed with streamers. No contest.

Vicki picked up the larger gift and smiled at Philippa. Philippa smiled back; she always did smile, even when Vicki scowled. She always lent Vicki money for the coffee machine, even though it was never repaid. She sent Vicki flowers on her birthday or if she were ill and thanked her profusely if Vicki remembered to send her a cheap card. Philippa knew Vicki was mean, yet was still her friend. A true friend.

"I hope you have a lovely Christmas, Philippa," Vicki said and meant it.

"I hope you do too," Philippa replied.

At home, Vicki didn't open the package.

Her neighbour had, as usual, invited everyone in the building round for a drink on Christmas morning. Until now, Vicki had always declined. To accept would mean she would be expected to offer something in return; something other than food or drink. This year she would go, and would give the pendant to her neighbour. She'd already given the better gift to Philippa; in the New Year, she would also offer her friendship.

16. Overlooked

Alan didn't like the way he looked. He no longer hated his lack of height; he had when he was a kid, but he'd got over it. At forty-three, he'd long since accepted that he'd never grow taller than five foot two and a quarter. His youthful looks also bothered him slightly less than they used to. His appearance did still worry him though; people hardly noticed him and never took him seriously. It wasn't only for himself that he worried, it was for his patients too.

When he'd first qualified, people were reluctant to allow him to treat them. Alan couldn't really blame them; he looked as though he'd barely completed senior school. No one could be blamed for doubting he'd completed medical training. Even after he became a senior surgeon, patients lacked confidence in his abilities.

"Have you ever done this op. before, doc?" nervous patients had asked.

"Several times, yes," he answered, knowing if he told them the truth, that he'd performed the technique hundreds of times, they'd think him a liar and be unable to trust him.

For a time, he'd carried around letters of thanks from grateful patients; he got plenty of those, because he was a very good doctor. They hadn't helped much and made him feel as though he were carrying a note from his mum.

It hadn't been all bad though. In some ways, his disappointing physical development had helped him. He never got picked on at school; the bullies literally overlooked him. Maybe he didn't seem worth the effort.

When his classmates had been hanging about on street corners, getting into trouble, Alan had gone down the library. He'd read every medical book he could find, hoping to find a way to increase his height. Although he didn't discover a growth formula, he developed an interest in biology and medicine. The studying helped him through exams he'd never expected to pass. Being unable to buy alcohol, without considerable fuss and embarrassment, had made sticking to his studies easier than for some of his friends.

"Coming for a drink, Al?" they'd ask after a lecture.

Alan would shake his head. The others would either have to wait whilst he returned to his digs for identification, or he'd have to ask one of them to go to the bar for him. "You go on; I want to write up my notes before I forget what was said."

Looking like a schoolboy hadn't made him very popular with the girls. They usually didn't notice him. When they did, they thought he was sweet, but wanted to go out with boys who were taller than them and who shaved. They did it nicely, but they usually turned him down. It'd hadn't been like that with Janet. She'd had a Saturday job in the grocery shop and he'd had to ask her to reach something for him. He'd been embarrassed, but she'd been really nice about it.

"It's not much better being tall you know. I have a job getting clothes to fit and people are always asking, 'what's the weather like up there?' And I bang my head on things."

"How tall are you?" he'd asked.

"Six foot two."

"That is tall."

"I know," she pointed out.

"Sorry, yes of course you do."

"What about you, then?"

"Five two and a quarter."

"You're kidding?" She'd laughed as she said it.

"It's not funny."

"Sorry, no your height isn't. It's just that there's exactly a foot difference. I'm actually six two and a quarter."

"I suppose you kept quiet about the quarter so as not to scare me off?"

"Something like that."

"Well, as I've not been scared off, would you come out with me?"

She'd agreed. They hadn't pretended the height difference didn't exist. Instead they'd joked about it. It had been a relief to talk about it to someone who understood. Janet hadn't minded that he looked younger than her either.

"Maybe it'll rub off on me," she'd said, or later, "My friends are all jealous, they think I've got a toy boy."

Alan explained his frustration when patients wanted an older looking doctor. "It's really annoying. For most people, looking young would be an advantage, but not for a doctor."

"Don't worry, you'll keep getting older and eventually it will show."

"I suppose."

"Look on the bright side, when your colleagues look as though they'd be too old to remember what to do, you'll still be looking in your prime."

She'd been right of course and Alan tried to accept his lot, without wishing his life away.

Going grey hadn't been any consolation. Alan's already fair hair had just looked a little blonder. However, it had been his hair that had finally provided the look of maturity he'd craved. Or rather the lack of hair had compensated for his lack of inches and apparent lack of years. Aged forty-three, and a quarter, Alan had developed a bald patch. The best bit was that, as his newly shiny head was below most people's eye level, he could be sure everyone would notice it.

17. A Spy In Our Midst

I can't remember who first told me Mrs Burton was a spy. I don't suppose anyone came right out and said it; I wouldn't have believed them if they had. She didn't look like a spy, but then you wouldn't be much of a spy if you did, would you? I didn't look like one either, but at fourteen I knew that's what I was destined for. I'd never missed an episode of Spooks and I'd watched every 007 DVD. I'd even read some of the books.

Mum told me I had to be extra polite to Mrs Burton. I have to be nice to all the old people who live in our road as it's a warden controlled area and Mum is the warden. It's not as bad as it sounds. For one thing it's easy for Mum to get to work and because of all the old people there are loads of buses so it's easy for me to get to school; or anywhere else when, as is usual, I don't want to go to school. Mum gets paid and we have our own house. There's just us.

"It would really help me if the residents liked you, Luke," she said.

Made sense, she works for the old folk, so in a way they're her boss. You don't cheek your boss or play tricks on him, so I couldn't do that with the people on our street. Once they got used to having a teenager about the place, some of them became my boss too. Although they could have their grass cut and gardens kept tidy for them, weirdly some of them liked to do their own gardening. Sometimes they'd pay me to mow the grass or some digging. It wasn't great money, but way better than getting up in the middle of the night for a paper round. I often got cake and sweets too. They'd do that even when I wasn't working for them.

Some of the old people liked to talk to me. At first I tried to avoid that; I didn't want to hear a lot of boring stuff about arthritis. I was especially worried about Ted Holmes; he had a limp. Mum asked me to go round and change a light bulb for him. She'd been on her way to do it when somebody's buzzer went. As I'd just been complaining I was bored, I couldn't say I had something better to do, so I did as Mum wanted.

"Thank you so much, lad," Ted Holmes said. "I'd do it myself, except I can't climb with this leg."

Spies, even fourteen-year-old trainee ones, are observant and I noticed the leg Ted tapped wasn't the one that dragged a little when he walked. "I thought your other leg was more painful, Mr Holmes?" I asked. Tactful eh?

He laughed, which is a funny reaction for someone who's been caught out. "No lad, that one don't hurt at all." He rolled up his trouser leg. His clothes had two legs, but he didn't.

"It's false?" I asked very stupidly. People aren't built with bits of metal holding their shoes away from their knees. "How did you lose it?" Maybe that was a bit ruder, but it was less stupid.

"Flying accident. Well, I suppose landing accident would be more accurate."

Suddenly Ted Holmes was interesting. He'd been in the RAF. He hadn't been on a spying mission that time, but he'd done some pretty amazing stuff and I was still asking him questions about it when Mum came to tell me my tea was ready.

After that, I found out some of the other people had done interesting stuff too. One chap told me he'd been in a big band. It can't have been all that big as I'd never heard of it, but he could still play the trumpet quite well. One lady had been a police woman and she told me her job had been just like it was shown on Life on Mars. Another said she'd been one of the girls who was often seen being stretchered off on old Beatles clips. She had photos to prove it. Funny thing was that when they all told me about this stuff, I stopped thinking of them as just old and started to see them as interesting people. More interesting than me in a way, because although I was going to be amazing, I hadn't really done anything yet. You'll understand why when Mrs Burton moved in, I thought it was just possible she really had been a spy.

I kept a close eye on her and knew she was doing the same to me. Nothing in that, they all did to start with. Don't blame them, I was young, strong and and sharp-eyed and they weren't. It would have been easy for me to steal from them. It would have been stupid too though. I'd be an obvious suspect and it wasn't worth risking Mum's job. Besides, once I got to know some of them it wouldn't have felt right to take the little they had.

Mrs Burton was different from the others. She didn't talk about herself. She asked a lot of questions. The usual stuff; what did I want to do when I grew up and about school. She asked a lot more questions than most people, especially about my form tutor, Mr Davies. I couldn't answer very well as I hadn't been in for a while, but she got me curious. Mr Davies was new. Could teaching be a cover for something? I started going to school first thing so I could keep an eye on him at registration. I kept quiet about my plans to be a spy; you can't be too careful.

Everywhere I went, Mrs Burton seemed to appear. Several times she saw me mooching about in town at lunchtime.

"I'll get the bus back to school with you, I'm going that way."

She didn't say where she was going, but I ended back in double English, or double maths. It was uncanny how she always managed to do this on days when I had a double session of something, so I couldn't escape very quickly. Then she found out the mother of my maths teacher was someone she used to be friends with and sometimes asked me to take notes or books to her. She always asked me to do it on days I had a maths lesson.

"I don't want to put you out, dear," she said.

She didn't put me out, but she did make it impossible to get out of maths.

One day, I went to see Ted Holmes, and Mrs Burton was there. They started talking about the weather and Mrs Burton slid a newspaper over whatever they'd been looking at. All I got was a glimpse of sky, a black shape in the middle and something orange in one corner. Something similar happened a few days later. They were better at changing the subject, but I caught a glimpse of that picture again and papers with what looked like maths equations and chemical formulas. Next time I surprised them together, I heard the words 'titanium' and 'expansion'. That didn't seem to go with the conversation about hanging baskets they pretended to be in the middle of.

I was pretty sure titanium was a special metal and I knew someone who'd know for sure; my science teacher. So that was another lesson I was going to have to show up for.

"Well well, Luke Southern. So what's got you so interested in science all of a sudden?" he asked.

As he'd asked, I told him. "Titanium, sir."

"Titanium? And what do you know about titanium?"

He had me there. "Not much, sir. You said if I was to turn up at your class there was a chance I'd learn about something that would interest me, so I've come to learn about titanium."

"It's true, I did say that."

Luck was on my side and the rest of the class all said they wanted to learn about titanium too. You can't blame them; it had to be more interesting than a boring old science lesson. Titanium is pretty amazing stuff. It's light and strong, just the sort of thing you'd want for a spy plane. Of course! That orange thing in the picture I'd seen Mrs Burton hiding had been a wind sock.

Ted Hughes was telling me about a tour of duty he'd been on delivering a special plane. He mentioned Okanawa and then looked as though he wished he hadn't. Straight away he started talking about a completely different assignment. I pretended not to notice, but I remembered that name.

"Mum, do you know what Okanawa is?"

"Don't know, Luke love. Sounds like it might be a place in Canada."

Another lesson to attend then; Geography. Okanawa isn't in Canada, it's in Japan. I learnt that and some stuff about rivers. I also got presented with a great long list of assignments that I'd managed to not hand in. That was mostly because I'd not been there when they were handed out. One was about Japan. I rather wished I'd been there for that lesson and decided I'd try the homework assignment to see if it led to anything interesting. It did. There was some kind of RAF base there, years and years ago. That was another clue about Mrs Burton. About Ted Holmes too; he had to be in on whatever it was.

The next time I overheard the two of them talking it was something about SR 17. That had to be code for something. They covered it up by talking about blackbirds and starlings and things, but I wasn't fooled, they'd never shown an interest in bird watching before.

What with keeping an eye on my tutor Mr Davies, checking up on things I'd overheard and passing notes to the maths teacher I was spending quite a bit of time at school. Started to see that if I'd been going all along, I'd have had some of the answers earlier. Those codes and things I'd seen written down, some looked like chemical symbols and… Hang on a minute. What was in the notes I was passing? I decided if I got another, I'd steam it open.

A good thing about attending school was that I could look things up on the internet. I typed in Titanium, SR 17 and Okanawa. What I got was information on a spy plane called a Blackbird. There was a picture too and it was a double for the one Mrs Burton and Ted Holmes had been hiding. I went round his place as soon as I got out of school. He wasn't there, but I tracked him down at Mrs Burton's place.

"You've worked it out then?" she asked me.

That's when I realised I hadn't. OK, I knew what they'd been talking about but not why or which side they were on. Ted Holmes I was pretty sure about. I'd used his stories for a history assignment. I'd put a bit of work into it and didn't want it all wasted with a rubbish mark so I'd done some research. I'd got an A, but more importantly, Ted Holmes had checked out. There were reports about him and pictures of him at remembrance parades. I'd thought he'd been exaggerating, but actually the bloke was a proper hero and proper modest about it.

Mrs Burton though, I wasn't so sure about her. Right from the start I'd thought she was up to something. I decided to play it cool.

"I know a few things," I said.

"Including what went on in '66?"

My face must have made it clear that other than knowing it was the year Mum was born, I didn't know anything about 1966.

Ted Holmes told me some interesting things about the Blackbird. I can't tell you it all now, you never know who's listening. I can tell you there was no doubt which side the pair of them were on.

"So are you testing me out for my future career?" I asked after I explained how I pieced together the clues and worked out what was on the picture I'd seen.

"Not exactly. We were doing our best to ensure you had the chance of a career, by trying to get you interested in science and maths," Ted Holmes explained.

"And I suppose I was still trying to do the job I retired from ten years ago," Mrs Burton admitted.

"Once a spy, always a spy?" I asked.

"A spy? I wouldn't put it like that. I'm not sure what the proper, politically correct name is these days, but in my day, I was known as a Truant Officer."

18. Small Ones Are More Juicy

"You've been Tangoed," I say playfully slapping young Clementine's bottom. You'd have thought Miss Jaffer would have heard that one before, but she just smiles.

I'm really something in the world of advertising, so you'll understand why I'm so delighted with Clementine. Got plenty of va va voom, but she's really naïve. She actually believes low fat chocolate cake will help make her slim.

"Murray, it's 95% fat free, so I can go ahead," she tells me.

She has a slice each morning with her richer roasted, fuller flavoured, coffee whilst I explain our latest campaign.

'Our' is such a useful word, it makes dear Clementine think we're a team. Mr Bannister offered her another position with a higher salary. That was close, thought I'd lose her there. Luckily I didn't lose my head, explained that with Bannister she'd be nothing but a pretty little typist.

"It's the business that impressed him, that's why he bought it. He doesn't care about the staff. Go compare the two of us."

Working for, no with, me was different. I was teaching her all my skills. With me she'd progress to great things. "It's the real thing, sweetheart. The team works, and you've got to be in to win it. You know that."

Didn't tell her I'd have to hire two girls to get through all the work she somehow manages. Organisation she says, that's what she's good at. Learnt it from the Sunday glossies apparently. Reads all them articles on de-cluttering your life and developing inner potential. They write that she can improve herself. She reads and believes every word. That's not all she reads. She believes those shoes advertised in the supplements really will be the most comfortable she's ever worn. Or if by some unlikely chance she found better, her money would be refunded in full, no questions asked. She believes that those uncreasable skirts sold in three different lengths actually are stylish. Not passion, not fashion, if you ask me.

Clemmie turns eagerly to the horoscopes. Surely no one but a fool could swallow the idea that one twelfth the population were about to be unlucky with money but forget these problems when they fell in love by midweek.

There she is over by the vending machine. I'll have a chat with her, tell her about my new car. She'll be impressed and a man likes to be appreciated when he's doing well. Clementine will understand what a sound investment it is too, how necessary to my professional image. Not like that nag of a wife at home. A boost to my ego she said. Even asked if I wasn't just slightly too young for a mid life crisis and it would be difficult to get the baby buggy in. Must be that time of the month I suppose.

"Nice skirt, Clementine love. Is it new?"

"Yes, Murray, I bought it from a magazine. Do you like it?"

"I'm loving it." And this is true.

The skirt gives me just the reason I need to take a long lingering look at Clementine. Maybe she's not quite the best a man can get, but she'll do me. I'd like to let my fingers do some walking there, I can tell you. I'd thought her a bit of a frump before. Had the right attitude, couldn't do enough for me of course, but not really worth much of my attention. Now I see things have changed. "Go on give us a twirl."

She spins round, very agile she seems, I like that.

"Nifty on your feet aren't you?"

"It's these lovely new shoes, they're so comfortable. I've bought a pair in every colour, so I'll hardly ever need to wear ordinary shoes again."

"Getting a drink were you?"

"I was, but I've just lost my last pound in the machine."

"Please allow me."

I put in my own money. An investment of a different kind. Every little helps. "What would you like?"

"Diet iron-bru please, someone told me I was looking a bit pale today."

What a girl, so suggestible that a chance remark convinces her she's anaemic and an old advertising campaign still has the power to persuade her a combination of colouring and flavourings can do her good. Something she's eating or drinking must be powerful stuff though. That dumpy assistant I started with has blossomed into a very attractive young woman. I put a pound in for the 60p drink and pocket the difference. Simples!

Time I explained the benefits of being nice to me, I think. She might not be the brightest, but give the girl her due she is trying hard. She's there at every meeting taking it all in. If anything needs to be checked, she's there.

"I'll just ask Jeeves," she murmurs before she's right back with the answer.

She must have bought every product the firm has ever handled. She says she likes a touch of luxury every day, which is fair enough.

She drives the make of car we promote. "I'm a thinking person and I thought as I'm on my own, I only need a small car, not a driving machine."

She wears the clothes, the make-up, to good effect, she is every bit gorgeous. She eats the food that makes life taste better. We all use some of the brands of course, because of the discounts though. I mean, why pay more? The rest of us aren't brainwashed like dear Clementine.

She sounds like an advert too, every phrase she uses is either currently promoting our clients products or soon will be. She is sympathetic, listens when I tell her how little my wife understands me. I'm sure Clementine could understand me very well. It's good to talk and I talk her kind of language don't I?

Old Bannister's been chatting to her again. I'd better nip in the bud any thoughts of moving her loyalty to him. He's the managing director, and I don't want her getting ideas.

"You stick with me Clementine, love. Together we'll go further."

"Are you sure you're not just using me because I love the jobs you hate?"

"Calm down dear, it's just commercials."

"I don't want to just be an assistant, can't you give me more responsibility?"

"At some point in time I will."

"Why not just do it?"

"Remember, you can't hurry a Murray."

I'm just explaining that it's Mr Bannister wants to take advantage of her not me, when I knock over her silly stuffed toys, a kitten and a bird.

"Cat's know the difference," Clemmie mutters. "Murray, please pick up that penguin."

I retrieve the fluffy green object. "Well, that's different, but it's not a hen."

"Things are going to be different, all right."

I'm still trying to work out what she means when Old Bannister calls me into his office.

"Murray, sit down. I've been hearing all about your marriage problems. I think it would be best if you took a few weeks off to sort things out. Treat her well, remember mums are heroes."

"There's no need, and my work …"

"Don't worry about that, Clementine will take over your department, I'm promoting her because she's worth it. Walking advertisement that girl. She'll go far: the future's orange."

19. Once More For Luck

"And now back to the beginning and we'll do the whole routine one more time," Sandy, the fitness instructor, sang out gleefully.

I tried; honestly I did. I couldn't see for the sweat in my eyes so it's not my fault I turned left when everyone else went right.

Splat! The woman I'd crashed into was no slimmer than me. It must have looked like two walrus fighting on a beach, or do I mean sea-lions? Some kind of blubber-rich, cumbersome creature. I'm not at all sure the lycra made things any better.

"Come on, you're not going to get fit lying there, you two," Sandy bitched.

I swear the horrible cow would have kicked us if we hadn't somehow found the strength to crawl out of range.

"I really, really hate her," my fellow walrus wheezed.

I didn't even have breath for that, so just nodded. We managed to get back into step with everyone else and I thought I was doing pretty well.

Sandy the sadist, of course, had other ideas. "Come on, squeeze those arms on the bicep curls. Just 'cause you've got bingo wings doesn't mean you can just flap them around!"

I lurched and stumbled through to the end of the sequence.

"Wonderful work, ladies," Sandy chirped. "Just march in place, or skip if you prefer."

I'd have preferred to skip over there and slap her face, but didn't have the strength. I concentrated on shuffling my weight from one foot to the other instead.

"Well, that completes the warm up, ladies. Now it's time to stretch our muscles for the work ahead."

Warm up? Muscles? She had to be kidding me. OK, I was hot, but the very reason I was there was that I had blubber where muscles should be. Or that's what I thought! Soon my pitiful excuse for muscles began to shriek with pain. I didn't half wish I was a spy and she an enemy agent so I could confess all and end the torture.

"Right, now it's time for the fat burner!" Sandy gleefully announced.

My fat was already burning. As were the muscles I'd just discovered. And my skin, bones and throat.

Self-tanned, severely bleached, Sandy bobbed about in front of us. How dare she look so perky and so pert?

I'm sure I passed out at one point. I'd needed water. Really needed it. That energetic witch wouldn't let me catch my breath to swallow it though.

"Come on, march in place," she bellowed at me. "Hydration is no excuse for idleness."

What about the sudden death of the fitness instructor, I wondered. If I were to fall on her while she demonstrated a floor move, that'd be twenty-seven sweaty women and one cool-skinned bimbo put out of their misery.

"Last time!" she called. Believing that escapee from hell, I gave it all of the very little I had left.

"One more time for luck!" she said.

I could tell she thought that was clever – and how alone she was in that thought.

Eventually she uttered the most wonderful words in the English language, "It's time to cool down. More gentle moves now."

I slowed down and moved gently.

"I didn't say stop!" she called from the other side of the gym.

I hate those mirrors even though I never look in them.

"Now for the stretches."

I sighed with relief as I sank onto my mat. Oh the joy of lying still and stretching my poor overworked limbs. We listened to soothing music and breathed deeply; something I had no trouble with.

Sandy stood over the lady I'd crashed into. "Exhale slowly and ease your leg back."

She moved on to me. "Just a little farther."

I inched it back a fraction more.

Sandy actually smiled. "Good work." Then she instructed us to do the same with our other leg.

"And we're done," she said at last.

As I mopped my face with my towel and took a blissful glug of water, Sandy explained how much good we'd done our hearts and how many calories we'd burned off.

"Fantastic work out, wasn't it?" my new friend, the walrus, said.

"Wonderful!" I agreed.

We both thanked Sandy and said how much we were looking forward to next week.

20. Helping With Enquiries

"Come on, Mrs Read. Why don't you just tell us the truth and save everyone a lot of time and trouble?"

For a moment, I was tempted to tell the constable the facts. In a way, it would be a relief. Living a life of deception over the previous few weeks had been a strain; I'm basically a truthful person. Telling lies isn't in my nature, but what choice did I have? My family had expectations; I couldn't let them down.

Thoughtfully I sipped my tea. I had no idea how they'd got on to me. I'd expected to be spending the afternoon slumped on the sofa and enjoying the fruits of my labours. Admittedly, some of those labours had been aimed at deceiving people, but it never occurred to me they'd see through my activities. If it had, then perhaps I'd never have ended up sitting on a hard wooden chair, being questioned by a detective and constable.

They didn't let up on the interrogation, despite my claims of innocence. A pair of handcuffs and a truncheon were clearly displayed. I'm sure that was deliberate; to remind me what could happen if I didn't co-operate. Helping the police with their enquiries did have some advantages though; I could sit down quietly with a nice cup of tea, knowing my husband was clearing up the house. They hadn't got him and I knew that without his corroborating evidence, they had nothing on me.

"How did you fake the footprints, Mrs Read?"

"Which footprints, Officer?" I asked as innocently as possible.

It hadn't taken them long to understand they were fake. Perhaps they knew more than I'd realised.

"Maybe you can explain this?" The detective held up my disguise.

"It looks like a cloak of some sort," I answered. Although I was startled, I didn't let it show. Instead, I stared at the stains left on my fingers from the finger-print process.

"It is. It's your size, smells of your perfume and has a hair the same colour as yours on it."

"You could have planted that," I said, but I knew they hadn't. Forensic evidence would prove me guilty. It wasn't just the clothing I was worried about. That had been left in the same location as I'd used to store the merchandise. All that planning, distracting the attention of this surprisingly thorough detective team, the patient hours spent obtaining the goods and getting them ready for distribution: wasted. I thought I'd been clever, I had, but not clever enough for this lot.

Faced with the evidence, I almost confessed. If it had just been the kindly looking constable questioning me, I would have done.

I wasn't prepared to enlighten the detective though. He looked about seven and I could have sworn his smart looking uniform was straight out the box. He was playing it by the book and using all the classic techniques.

First, they'd tried the old good cop / bad cop routine. That didn't faze me; my kids are more alarming when they refuse to eat their sprouts than the smug looking detective managed to be. The constable's pleading didn't stand a chance of swaying me either. After giving birth to three kids, I'd learnt to be tough. Their least successful tactic was to leave me alone to stew. To be honest, I enjoyed the peace and quiet and they cracked long before I did.

"Mrs Read, you might as well confess. Your partner has already told us everything," the detective said as he returned.

They were bluffing, they had to be. A quick glance at the desk sergeant in the other room reassured me. His wink and the fact that he was being allowed to carry on with his tasks meant they didn't even suspect him. Funny that, for all their cleverness, they never considered I might have a man on the inside.

Their theories got a little wilder after that. They asked about some gang up north and whether I was protecting them. I said nothing. Next, they started talking about conspiracies. The way the talked, every adult in the western world was involved in a plot to deceive. I kept quiet.

It was my lawyer who finally made me confess. I overheard the detective coaching her. I didn't mind too much when I heard her barking out, "Objection, your honour!" but was a little concerned when they started discussing who was going to be the judge. My trial was to be rigged! My man on the inside was no match for a judge in their pocket.

A glance at my watch told me that *EastEnders* was due to start in just a half an hour. I had to do something to get them to release me.

"OK, OK, I confess."

The detective and his team wouldn't let it go at that though. I had to show them how I'd faked the footprints and explain the subterfuges I'd used to move the merchandise around. My faithful accomplice was trapped by their questioning; they soon realised I hadn't acted alone.

"Come on then, Mrs Read. For the record, let's have that confession one more time."

"I confess that I, Mrs Read, mother of Constable Read, Detective Read and Lawyer Read, conspired with Sergeant Read to deceive. We obtained goods which we hid and we faked snowy footprints. I disguised myself in a red cloak, to pretend that I was Santa Claus."

21. Who Ate All The Cakes?

I hurried into the tea room looking forward to a chocolate cake. One of those would go nicely with the mug of hot tea I so badly needed. Showing people around Solent Castle is a rewarding job, but at this time of year it's also bitterly cold. You need a bit of extra food to keep you going. We get it too. Almost every day someone brings in a cake, or biscuits, or buns.

That morning I'd brought in chocolate cup cakes. Not supermarket own label either, really classy ones with large chunks of white chocolate in the rich, buttery chocolate sponge. Each was topped with gooey dark chocolate ganache and a Belgian truffle. Bringing them into work seemed a sensible option, as if they'd stayed at home I'd have eaten the lot and I really didn't need to do that.

As I removed my wooly hat, scarf, gloves, coat and fleece I glanced at the table in the centre of the room. The plate was still there but it contained nothing but crumbs. There was no need to ask who'd eaten all my cakes; it would have been Stanley.

How it works in theory is that the goodies are put on a plate around ten thirty and everyone who fancies helps themselves to one during their first tea break. Whatever's left over is eaten on a first come first fed basis during the afternoon tea break. What happens in practice, whenever Stanley's shift are working, is we take one each during the morning and he eats whatever's left in his lunch break.

Stanley isn't terribly popular. He's nice enough in some ways. Always offers people a lift if the weather's bad and he'll swap shifts with anyone if they want a particular day off. He's a bit mean though, when it comes to money. Brings in his own teabags and drinks it black rather than pay into the tea fund. It's easy to guess whose name he draws for buying the Christmas gift as theirs will always be the cheapest. The few times he does bring in cakes they'll have reduced stickers on and be just past the sell by date.

The rest of us had talked about his habit of eating everything we brought in and plotted to spike cakes with laxative chocolate or chilli powder. I'd always thought that a bit mean, but as I drank my tea and looked at the plate which had once held those, oh so delicious, cakes I changed my mind. I cheered myself up imagining the worst things to put in a pie and leave for him.

Stanley came in just as I'd decided on curried sprouts, candied peel and licorice all topped off with coffee icing and a cherry. I pointedly mentioned how hungry I was.

"I know the feeling," he said as he picked up the empty plate. "Sorry I just left this, but Marian was leaving for her dentist appointment and found her bike tyre was flat. By the time I'd fixed it I didn't have time for lunch so just grabbed the last two and went back to work."

I couldn't exactly moan when he'd given up his lunch break to help someone, could I? Just to make me feel even worse, after he'd washed the plate, he offered me one of his sandwiches. They were limp white bread with the thinnest sliver of what I guessed was ham. Stanley's reluctance to spend money included any purchases for himself. He never went away on holiday, instead spending his time with cousins. His clothes and car were the same ones he'd had when I'd first started working at the castle and they'd been old then.

"Sheila?" he said. "I was thinking of bringing my cousin and the kids in tomorrow. I wondered if you could show them how the spit works?"

"Yeah, sure." It was standard practice for us to bring in friends and family for free when it was quiet and we'd ask the other staff to give them a bit of an extra show. I often demonstrate cookery as it would have been done in the castle. It's great to light the fire in the winter and roast a chicken or piece of meat and share it amongst visitors.

It occurred to me he'd asked for that instead of a demonstration of weaving or falconry so he'd save money on feeding them all, but maybe that was harsh. People do love to see the spit and the weather just then made it even more appealing.

Whenever Stanley talked about his family it seemed like he was holding something back, so we'd all assumed they must be rich and Stanley spent time with them for what he could get out of them. One look showed me that wasn't the case. They weren't dressed a whole lot more smartly than Stanley. All of them were quiet and tired looking. Maybe that wasn't surprising as the twelve of them couldn't have been comfortable in Stanley's flat.

It was easy to see why he was so keen on them though. As you might have guessed, Stanley doesn't get a lot of admiration from his colleagues but this lot treated him like he was royalty or something. Maybe they thought he was? They were foreign and one of the adults had to translate everything I said. The kids looked up at him as though he was Santa and those who spoke English kept thanking him, and then me, for our kindness

Stanley looked uncomfortable. Something was definitely up. Maybe he'd charged them for coming in, possibly even more than the normal entrance fee for special access or something like that?

When the kids were all busily eating chunks of roasted lamb and bread I pulled Stanley to one side. "Are these really all your cousin's children?" I demanded.

"In a way."

"Either they are or they aren't."

"She runs an orphanage in Chernobyl and these children all come from there."

"Oh." There had been a bit in the paper about how everything around Chernobyl was still contaminated with radiation. Food and water had to be imported, making it expensive, but still people got sick more than they should. I'd meant to send a few pounds. Stanley brought in that paper. I remembered because usually he read someone else's.

"Is it really as bad out there as it said in the paper?"

"Worse. I was sending money to help, but found out that what they really need is to get away. Spending time away from the radiation, even just for a few weeks, can help them get stronger and live years longer. So whenever I get a holiday from work I invite them over."

"And you pay for it all?"

"As much as I can, but it's not enough. There's a charity which helps. They cover most of the travel expenses and arrange for the kids to see a doctor and dentist while they're here."

Things have changed at work now. Stanley still eats most of the food we bring in, but there's a lot less of that now. Instead of bringing in so many cakes and biscuits, each week we all drop change into a collection box for the charity which helps Stanley's children. Instead of giving each other silly gifts for Christmas we send out a food parcel for the children. It's not all one way though. At least once a month we get a painting or letter from them. That's better for our waistlines than cakes and biscuits and it warms us better than a mug of tea.

22. Fred's Hat

Frederick McCilroy studied himself in the mirror. He appeared exactly what he was; a newly qualified doctor with little experience. Maybe he should have tried to grow a moustache before joining the rural practice? No point worrying about that just before he was due to make his first house call.

He wanted to help people and make a difference, but from what he'd experienced that morning he knew it would be difficult to gain his patients' trust. He overheard one patient say to the receptionist, "In future I only want to see one of the doctors, not a lad fresh from college."

Fred needed something to reassure people. As he strode down the Hight Street, medical bag in hand, he saw it; a hat. It was the kind of tweed deerstalker popular with the older generation of the small town. The sort of hat worn by his recently retired predecessor. He tried it on and paid for in less than two minutes. Fred was certain it made him look more mature and it definitely boosted his confidence.

Luckily for him, his next patient's condition was painful but easily treated. Even more fortunately the lady was a real gossip and very grateful to Fred. Word quickly spread about the talented new doctor.

When he'd served the community for a few years, a young patient came to see him with a very minor complaint.

After examining him Fred said, "I think you know as well as I do that this isn't serious and will clear up of its own accord in a few days." He was puzzled. Billy was due to leave for university in a few weeks; to study biology. He was a clever student. Fred knew as he'd helped coach him in his spare time.

"I thought so, but just wanted to be sure."

"Ah." Fred understood. It was his patient's mind, not his body that was troubling him. He remembered his apprehension on coming to the town and recognised it in Billy "I was nervous when I first came here you know, but I got over it."

After he'd explained about his hat, Fred went into the hall and fetched it. "Would you like to have it?"

"Really?" He took it. "Thank you."

Billy loved the hat. To him it wasn't just a piece of clothing but a symbol. It proved to him Dr McCilroy, whom he greatly admired, had faith in him. He already knew his family and teachers thought he had the ability to succeed. Knowing an outsider felt the same way was a big boost. He was determined to work hard and not let any of them down.

Billy graduated with an excellent degree and went on to become a teacher. The hat went with him when he took up his first post and gave him confidence. Billy was a good teacher, respected by colleagues and students alike.

Years later, when the hat had long been consigned to the cupboard under the stairs, Billy acted as mentor to a student teacher. Paul was clever, funny and enthusiastic. He was also so nervous the pupils never appreciated these points.

"You need to show a little authority," Billy told him. "The pupils need to be led to some extent. You don't want to bully them or push them around of course, but neither can you let them do that to you."

"I know you're right, but they just don't listen to me."

Much the same was said in the staffroom that lunchtime, when Paul was on playground duty. "How can he teach if the children just talk over him?" someone asked.

"He'll be fine once he gets a bit of confidence," Billy said.

"If he ever does."

The next day Billy told Paul the history of his old hat. "You're welcome to it."

"I don't suppose it can do any harm. Thanks." Paul took the carrier bag and looked inside. "Oh a deerstalker! I'm a real Sherlock Holmes fan."

"What you got on yer 'ead?" a pupil asked Paul in the first break.

Paul smiled as he remembered they boy's name. "Come and take a loo… Watson isn't it?"

"Yeah."

As the boy stepped closer, Paul saw a group of his classmates standing a little way off. They were laughing and Paul guessed that, though he'd seemed cocky, young Watson had probably been egged on to say something about the hat.

Paul told the boy about Sherlock Holmes' incredible detecting abilities and about his assistant. He laid stress on Watson's intelligence, bravery and strength. As he described some of the adventures the duo had shared, Paul noticed the other boys drawing nearer to find out what was going on. By the time the bell for lessons sounded he was surrounded by a group of interested boys.

When those same boys appeared in the classroom, chatting loudly amongst themselves Paul said, "I'm going to try an experiment if that's OK?"

Billy told him to go ahead.

Paul called Watson to the front of the class and quietly asked him if he'd be his assistant during the lesson.

"What d'you want me to do?"

"Just hand out the textbooks and things and collect them up later. Not just yet though."

Gradually the room grew quiet as the boys wondered what Paul was saying to Watson this time. As Watson distributed textbooks, Paul told them that gathering knowledge was like searching for clues which would help them solve problems later in life. Either that advice or his promise to read a Sherlock Holmes mystery on Friday, if they worked hard, persuaded the boys to pay attention to the lesson.

Once Paul gained the children's interest he had no trouble keeping it. By the end of term he was well on the way to becoming an excellent teacher. By then the hat was shabby and he took it out to the bin. As he lifted the lid, to drop the hat in, a gust of wind sent it over the low fence. It landed at the feet of his neighbour's daughter.

"Don't you want that?" Melanie asked.

"No, I'm having a bit of a clear out."

"Can I have it?" It would be perfect for Saturday's fancy dress party. She'd been invited by a former college friend but had been reluctant to go. She was shy and dressing up made her feel even more uncomfortable, but she could hide in her dad's discarded gardening jacket and pull the flaps of the hat down over her face.

"Of course."

So safe did Melanie feel, hidden in her outfit that when a young man she vaguely recognised from college offered her a drink she not only accepted, but also replied to his questions with more than one word answers.

"What is it you've come as?" he asked.

"I haven't really decided if I'm a farmer or a scarecrow."

"Farmer I think, you're not very scary."

"No, I suppose not." She wasn't scared either.

"Just as well, or I might not have had the nerve to talk to you."

"Oh." So the reason he'd not spoken to her before was nothing to do with him not liking her. She told Marty how she'd acquired the hat and that, if she hadn't, she probably wouldn't have gone to the party.

"Well I'm glad you did. What are you going to do with it now?"

"Throw it away, I suppose. It's pretty tatty." She took it off.

"Still warm though, I should think?"

"Very."

"Could I have it? There's this homeless guy I pass on the way to work and the weather isn't getting any better."

"Please do give it to him." Melanie offered the hat.

"Keep it for now or you'll get cold going home. Maybe I could come for it in the week and we could go for a drink?"

"I'd like that."

The date with Melanie was a success. He went home with the hat and the promise he'd see her again the following weekend.

Marty worked as a reporter for the local newspaper and saw some of the best and the worst that could happen to people. One minute he could be interviewing a lottery winner, the next doing a piece on a tragic death. After just an hour or so talking to a person he often knew almost their whole life history.

He'd chatted to the homeless man several time, yet still knew almost nothing about him. Marty had no idea what had happened to leave him sleeping rough. Perhaps bad luck, maybe bad decisions or even actions. Whatever the reason he didn't think Fred was a bad person. Marty had done a few articles about the homeless people living in the town and heard stories about Fred. Other homeless people claimed he'd helped them with their problems. He'd once performed CPR on a commuter, saving his life. The grateful man had given him a cash reward. The only good that did Fred was to allow him to sit inside and drink instead of swigging from a bottle in the street.

Marty wouldn't give the man money, knowing that too would just go on drink, but he gave him food sometimes. Fred always thanked him and ate it, but refused offers of a place in the local shelter. It had been a while since Marty had tried to get him to go there though and, as he'd told Melanie, the weather was getting worse.

Fred watched the young man approach. He'd been like him once, thinking he could help people. He had too, but he hadn't been able to help his darling wife. The cancer took her, then whisky claimed him. His drunkenness hadn't caused him to prescribe the wrong drugs, or miss symptoms of a serious condition but only through luck and the vigilance of his colleagues. They'd supported him as long as they could, but he'd had no interest in sobering up and continuing with his life. Now it was probably too late.

"Here, this is for you," Marty said. He gave Fred a plastic cup of hot soup and a packet of sandwiches.

"Thanks." He ate and drank.

"Please, Fred, let me take you to the shelter. I'm worried

about you in the cold."

"Don't feel it much," Fred indicated the paper-wrapped bottle by his side.

"That's no good. Alcohol will make you more likely to die from the cold."

"Yes, I know. I used to be a doctor." Now why had he said that? He didn't usually offer any personal information. In fact he'd only ever revealed his former profession when he'd realised someone was in urgent need of medical attention and hadn't been able to convince them to get it without revealing the truth.

"Then let me help you. Please."

Fred shook his head.

"Well at least take these." Marty offered a pair of gloves and a scarf he'd got in a charity shop and the hat Melanie had given him.

"I used to have a hat like that. Made me feel I was somebody, that I could help people."

"You are somebody. You do help people and you could help me."

"How's that?" Fred asked.

"There's this girl. I like her and she'll think I'm a hero if I persuade you into that shelter and to seek help."

Fred had been a hero once, in a way. Some of his patients owed him their lives. That young student Billy had idolised him, and his wife had truly loved him. Maybe he did deserve a hot shower, comfortable bed and a little hope.

Fred pulled on his old hat. "Come on then, help me up."

23. Not Paying Attention

"… enjoy some warmth and a well earned break," Kiri finished in reply to what she'd caught of her client's complaining conversation about her son going away to Australia.

"What a horrible thing to say!" Coral screeched at Kiri, making her drop the box of curlers.

"I'm sorry, Coral." Kiri tried to sound apologetic, even though she had no idea what she'd done wrong. As she scrabbled about on the floor, trying not to collect snippets of hair with the curlers, her client continued to shout.

"And don't be impertinent! It's Mrs Jenkins to you. Just because Charles calls me Coral doesn't mean a bit of a girl like you can do it."

Hearing his name, Charles, in his trademark head-to-toe skinny black, stalked over to see what the fuss was about. Kiri knew she was in trouble again, but had no idea what she'd done wrong.

"This… this girl was saying she didn't blame my son for emigrating to Australia. She was implying he was right to do it to avoid me."

Actually, now she knew the facts, Kiri was starting to think exactly that. It wasn't what she'd meant though. For a start she'd assumed he was just taking a holiday.

"I'll take over here," Charles said. "Kiri, you fetch Coral a cup of tea and then take a turn on reception." With a delicate gesture, he shooed her away.

"Yes, Charles." She scurried away, half annoyed at being given what was really the Saturday girl's job and half relieved to get away from Coral Jenkins. The woman was a misery at the best of times.

Once Charles had set Coral's hair, he motioned for Kiri to follow him to his office.

"What was that all about?" he asked.

"I just misunderstood what she said. You know I wouldn't be deliberately rude to a customer, even one who deserved it as much as she does."

"What you mean is you were in a world of your own again and didn't listen to a word she said?"

"Umm …" OK as soon as Coral had mentioned Australia, Kiri's mind had wandered to warm sunshine, snorkelling in crystal clear water and seeing kangaroos hopping across the outback. She'd imagined herself flirting with a bronzed surfer dude. She could take a gap year out there, cutting hair to pay her way. All she'd need was a chair set up on the beach and a good pair of scissors. Those surfer boys wouldn't want to go into stuffy salons, but once they saw how quick and efficient she was they'd be queuing up for trims. That would be much better than…

"Kiri, are you listening to me?"

"Yes, Charles. You were saying I should pay more attention." It was a good bet as that's what he was usually telling her.

"Give it a try will you? Please."

Fortunately a very reluctant young lad was dragged in soon afterwards. He'd been in before, refused to have his hair washed and squirmed so much the stylist dealing with him nearly cut his ear off.

"Your chance to redeem yourself," Charles said.

The boy, who was wearing a T-shirt decorated with dinosaurs sat as good as gold listening to the tale Kiri told him about trimming the hair of woolly mammoths. "Gets into terrible knots if they don't put anything on it," she said. "I'll squirt a bit of the stuff we use on them onto your head once I've washed your hair so you can see what it's like, OK?"

"OK."

By the time he had short, tidy and shiny hair she'd told him about dyeing the feathers of pterodactyls to help them with camouflage.

"I didn't fink they had feathers?"

She knew he, very sensibly, didn't believe a word Kiri was saying, but as he was behaving and having fun, she continued. "A lot don't. They're allergic to the dye. It makes them itch so much they rub the feathers right off."

Kiri moved on to telling him about how a stegosaurus invented the mohican cut as she washed his mother's hair. She quickly teased the woman's sudsy locks into the appropriate shape to aid the explanation.

As she snipped she discussed painting the toenails of a Diplodocus, "It's two and a half bottles for each one and you have to work really fast or they get bored, go to sleep, fall over and smudge it."

"Then do the other dinosaurs laugh?"

"Oh gosh, yes. The trachodons especially. Laugh at anything they will." She was glad his Mum's hair was almost done as she'd used up all the dinosaur names she could see written on the boy's shirt.

"Thank you so much," his mother said, handing Kiri a generous tip. She took one of the salon's leaflets and circled Kiri's name. "So I know who to ask for in future."

Charles nodded approvingly and it seemed the earlier misunderstanding had been forgiven if not forgotten. Her employer had more reason to be pleased with her the following weekend. A customer came in with two unruly little girls, saying Kiri had been recommended.

It didn't take Kiri long to discover they were both pony mad. She told them the protective capes, used to keep clients' clothes dry and free from hair, were stable rugs. Once they had them on, she called them Dobbin and Treacle and said she was getting them ready for a gymkhana. They behaved perfectly the whole time. Afterwards, Kiri talked Charles into buying child-sized capes in a range of colours. He'd raised one tidy eyebrow at the suggestion not everyone felt comfortable wearing black, but admitted children weren't really his area of expertise.

As the weeks went by, more and more children were brought in. The parents always asked for Kiri. Sometimes dads joined in with the storytelling. Often mothers, once they saw their child would be content to wait, decided to have their own hair cut as well.

Coral Jenkins still came in for her weekly wash and set. Kiri was pleased the woman would overhear mothers asking for Kiri and saying how kind and friendly she was. Hopefully that'd give her something to think about.

One day Coral suddenly laughed very loudly and said to Charles, "Oh dear, I've spoken without thinking again. I do sometimes If I have something on my mind, but I don't mean any harm."

Kiri glanced over and saw Coral looking straight at her.

The remark was probably Coral's idea of an apology.

Several times after that Kiri felt the woman staring at her and occasionally it looked as though she was about to speak. Kiri always got in first with a cheery, "Good morning, Mrs Jenkins," or "Lovely weather, Mrs Jenkins". She then immediately turned her attention to a job as far away from Coral as she could manage. It wasn't just that she didn't want a row, she also didn't want to cause more upset to a woman who clearly had enough troubles.

Thankfully Kiri didn't need the aid of her imagination to look busy or keep herself occupied as she was often in demand. Charles's takings and Kiri's tips reached an all time high over the Easter holidays.

"Kiri, there's someone who'd like to speak to you," the Saturday girl said, the following week.

Kiri looked over and saw Coral Jenkins standing by the reception desk. "It's not me she wants. Tell Charles that Mrs Jenkins is waiting, will you? He'll deal with her." She turned her attention back to her client and spritzed on a little more spray.

Coral was still waiting when the customer had paid and booked her next appointment.

"Mrs Jenkins, I'll ask Charles to …"

"No, please. It's you I want to talk to." She looked almost nervous.

"I've got a tea break in a few minutes. I'll just grab a coffee and come out." Kiri had no idea what mischief Coral had in mind this time, but didn't intend to go without coffee in order to find out.

"Can you meet me in the cafe? I'll go and order you a drink. My treat."

Charles had appeared to see what Coral wanted. He must have overheard as he said, "Go now if you like, Kiri. You've been very busy so you needn't come back until ten past three. I'll get someone else to wash your next client's hair."

Glad as she was of an extended break, Kiri could have done without Coral just then. She had indeed been very busy and didn't have the energy to be extra tactful with Coral and she was sure she'd have to be, even if the woman had come to apologise. Kiri grinned; if she thought Coral had come to say sorry she really was letting her imagination run away with her.

A large latte and selection of cakes awaited Kiri when she stepped into the cafe.

"I didn't know what you'd like. Please have a seat."

"What is it you wanted to speak to me about, Mrs Jenkins?"

"Well, I suppose it's about David."

"Who is David?" Kiri was pretty sure she didn't know any Davids. At least, not in a way Coral could object to.

"My son. We had an argument after, well after …"

Kiri just stopped herself from saying, "After you shouted at me?" and changed it to, "After our misunderstanding?"

"Er, yes. He said I never listen to him because I'm always letting my imagination run away with me thinking the worst of everyone and everything."

Kiri didn't know what to say, so she took a large bite of cream slice. Escaping into her imagination made sense for Kiri as hers was a lovely place to be. Coral's sounded awful.

"He was right. I oh, I'm doing this all wrong. I meant to apologise. You weren't being deliberately rude, I knew that. You just misunderstood what I'd said."

Kiri nodded. She almost admitted that was partly her fault as she'd not been listening, but she wasn't sure that would be a good idea.

A tear spilled down Coral's cheek. "I don't know how to make it all right. I was horrible."

Kiri eyed the plate of cakes and imagined herself eating the chocolate eclair and perhaps taking that bit of shortcake back for later. If Coral paid for the lot she'd be more than forgiven. She gave herself a mental shake; hadn't she promised herself to pay attention? Coral wouldn't be this upset, weeks later, over their falling out. There must be more to this. What could it be? Maybe she was dying and wanted to make peace with as many people as possible first, or perhaps her son had been eaten by a crocodile. Or maybe she should just ask, instead of letting her fantasies get her into trouble again.

Before she could, Coral thanked her for listening and being so understanding. As she followed that with, "I'll just go and pay the bill," Kiri smiled and assured her it was no problem.

As Kiri was congratulating herself on a job well done, even if she hadn't really done anything at all, Coral said, "I'll see you on Saturday then."

Help. Coral always had her hair set on Wednesday as that was the half price day for pensioners. If she was coming in on a Saturday it must be for something special. Kiri refused to let herself imagine what Coral thought she'd agreed to and all the ways it could go wrong. She did think of going sick, but Saturday was the busiest day and they had a bridal party booked. Without Kiri there, customers with appointments would be turned away. That wouldn't be fair.

The bridal party arrived as soon as the salon opened.

Normally Kiri would have fantasised about being a bride herself, or maybe a guest would be better as she could flirt with a handsome usher and have all the romance still to come. This time though, she hardly gave the champagne, luxurious food and slow dances a thought.

She kept her attention fully on the job until Coral arrived. Mrs Jenkins had a small boy by the hand and looked very nervous. Had she kidnapped him to take the place of her son?

"Do I have Mrs Jenkins booked in?" Charles asked the Saturday girl, although he must know he didn't.

"No, there's no Mrs Jenkins booked at all, today."

"That's right," Coral said. "The appointment is for Joshua and it's with Kiri. Joshua, this is the nice lady I was telling you about."

"And this young man is …?" Clearly Charles was as mystified as Kiri as to why the woman with just one son, who was in Australia, would have a child with her.

"This is my grandson. He's David's boy. You remember I mentioned my son last time I was here?"

Charles and Kiri agreed they did remember.

"Well he's in Austria at the moment."

"Austria?" Kiri asked. "Not Australia?"

"Yes, that's right. He's working there for three months, but Joshua and his mum are staying here."

"I see," Charles said. He said what a fine boy Joshua was and left Kiri to deal with him.

Kiri thought she understood why Coral had been upset before, she'd misunderstood what her son had said and jumped to the worst possible conclusion. Realising Kiri had the same tendency not to pay attention and instead retreat into her imagination, Coral had lashed out at her own failing. This time Kiri absolutely, definitely would pay attention.

"So, what are we doing with your hair, Joshua?"

"Granny said it has to be tidy."

"Tidy is good. That way you'll know where to find it."

Joshua giggled. "Could it really get lost? Is that why some men have no hair?"

"I'm not sure, but I don't think we should risk it. Now you go and see if one of those capes will fit you and we'll get started."

As he went to look at the box of brightly coloured capes the Saturday girl had ready, Kiri said to Coral, "I didn't know you had a grandson."

"I hardly do myself. I had a row with David when he said he was moving in with Sonia, that's David's mother. I refused to talk to her. So stupid, I realise now."

"And they didn't tell you about Joshua?" She knew Coral was difficult, but that seemed very harsh.

"They did. He was two when David met Sonia and I thought she was just using him as a meal ticket. David loves him as his own though and asked me to keep an eye on them both while he was away and… well you know the rest."

"Now you're here with him I do. Obviously you've made it up with them."

"I'm trying. I don't know how to start though. You're good with children. I was hoping you'd have some suggestions."

Oh, so that's why Coral had wanted to talk to her. Kiri felt bad for never giving her the chance.

Joshua reappeared at that moment, wearing a bright red cape.

"Good choice," Kiri said. "I like red." She showed him her fingernails. "When I was little I liked playing snakes and ladders and other games with my gran and I always wanted to have the red counter."

"That stuff is booooooring," Joshua said.

"I suppose you prefer outdoor things?"

"Yes, like riding my bike. My bike is red." Then his cheery smile vanished. "I'm not allowed to ride it while Daddy is away. Mummy says it's not safe on the roads on my own."

Kiri had to agree with that. This wasn't going at all well. Neither was Joshua's haircut. She'd better get on with it. The sooner he was gone, the less damage her chatter might cause.

"I didn't know about your bike, Joshua," Coral said. "Perhaps you could bring it to my house."

Oh no! If Coral tried to go against what the boy's mother said, especially when it concerned his safety, then things were only going to get worse.

"And ride it on your road?" Joshua demanded.

"No, Mummy is right that's not safe. You could ride it in the park."

That was better. Or it would be if the local park wasn't so tiny. She guessed that laps of the circular track might soon get booooring on his own. Kiri firmly pushed away an image of Coral racing him on a pink, child's tricycle.

"Then I could go really fast!"

"I have a stopwatch," Coral said. "I could time you and see if you beat any records."

"That's a great idea!" Kiri said. "What other things do you like doing?"

"Eating cakes!"

"And what does Mummy think about that?" Kiri, remembering the plateful Coral had bought for her, quickly asked. She didn't want Coral to promise treats his mum wouldn't approve of. Especially as a young woman was now sat in reception watching them. Her hair was the same red-gold as Joshua's, her eyes were exactly like his and she was carrying a bright red coat in just his size.

"Mummy likes cakes. She likes eating anything she doesn't have to cook!"

The young woman's expression confirmed it was her the boy was talking about. Even with all the mirrors, Coral wouldn't see her from where she was stood. Should Kiri try to alert her somehow?

"I like cakes too," Coral said. "I like cooking them and eating them."

"Your gran is great at giving people cake. She gave me some and it was lovely. That was just a practice for taking you and your mum out. She's really looking forward to it."

"Are you?" asked the young woman, who had approached as Kiri's attention was divided between her words and Joshua's fringe.

Coral spun round and drew in a sharp breath. "Yes, Sonia, I am. I'm looking forward to that and to getting to know you and Joshua much better."

"What a lovely thing to say," Sonia said.

Kiri breathed a sigh of relief and then started to wonder if she'd ever have a mother-in-law who took her out for cakes. Perhaps they'd go shopping together and stop for refreshments, or maybe she'd bake them. That would be best. Kiri could trim her hair while they cooked and…

24. A New Broom

It seemed to Sara that she was the only person to have a good word to say about the new manager. Maybe, as his assistant, she was biased in his favour?

"Donald shouts at me and says I'm lazy," Phil said. "You know I'm not well, it's not fair to pick on me."

"Of course not, Phil. I'll have a word with him," Sara soothed.

Personally she thought all that was wrong with Phil was the shock of being expected to do a whole day's work from Monday to Friday. The previous manager had let him get away with arriving late most days, leaving early just as frequently and doing very little in between.

"He says I'm stupid and can't spell anything," Tina said.

"There's no call for him to do that," Sara comforted her. Tina wasn't the brightest light on the Christmas tree, and needed guidance, but being rude to her wasn't going to help anyone.

"He only got the job because he's married to the boss's daughter," Tina claimed.

Maybe the family relationship had helped a bit, but Donald possessed good qualifications, appropriate experience and had greatly improved both the quality and quantity of work produced by his staff. He wasn't going to be able to keep that up though if he continued to upset them. Sara had promised to have a word with him and it looked as though that was the best course of action for all their sakes.

Sara was on her way to his office, when the new cleaner bumped into her. The poor girl was crying noisily.

"He touched me," she sobbed.

How dare he! Sara took the girl to the rest room and made her a cup of tea. She was too upset to explain to Sara what he'd done, but from the way she was trembling it had to have been bad. Sara felt angry with him, but even more with herself for having defended such a horrible man.

When Donald went to a meeting, she gathered the staff together and said, "We'll have to do something about him, anyone have any ideas?"

They didn't, but promised to back her up if she thought of a plan.

Donald came back from his meeting and briefed everyone about the matters that had been raised. He was so calm and professional she decided she'd over reacted earlier. Maybe there had been some kind of misunderstanding and if she reasoned with him, he'd find a way to put things right.

The minute she stepped into his office, she realised her mistake.

"What's up?" he said.

Clearly he expected her to have a complaint; why would he think that if he'd done nothing wrong? When she explained her concerns he dismissed them as lies saying the staff were conspiring against him.

"Sara, most of that is wildly exaggerated at best. The staff simply aren't used to working to a high standard and for sustained periods and are putting more energy into gathering together and complaining than adapting to the perfectly reasonable new regime."

"It's not just the staff who worked for the old manager who're unhappy …"

"That little madam was asking for it," he declared before Sara even mentioned the cleaner.

He had to go. Sara didn't approve of dirty tricks, but she couldn't think of anything more subtle than blackmail to get rid of him. The end would justify the means. He really did deserve what she was about to do. It really wasn't at all relevant that she was next in line for promotion and likely to get his job if he left.

She started by returning to Donald's office and pretending to believe his conspiracy theory. She invited him for a drink as a belated welcome into the department. Anyone with any sense would have seen through that, but he was either so ready to badmouth the others, or so intent on treating her as he had the cleaner, that he agreed.

Phil was waiting in the bar, camera at the ready, when she and Donald walked in. Sara made a point of straightening Donald's tie and accidentally brushing her hand against his. Phil selected and printed the shots which appeared the most incriminating.

Sara's next move was to book herself into the honeymoon suite of a classy hotel, using Donald's surname. For the two nights he was away at a conference, she was alone at the hotel. It cost her almost a month's salary, but the expected promotion would make up for that.

Donald returned from the conference to find Sara in his office. She handed him photographs and a photocopy of the hotel bill.

"These are copies. You can have the originals if you leave the department and give me a reference that'll help me get your job."

"Don't be silly, Sara. You know I've done nothing wrong."

"Do you think your wife and father-in-law will believe you?"

In less than a month, Donald had the 'evidence' and Sara had his job. On her first day in her new role, the staff were jubilant. They cheered as she walked into the office and presented her with a plant for her desk.

Sara decided her first task was to tackle the regular customer newsletter. Donald had moaned it took days to do and what a chore it was to get right, so she'd better make a start whilst she was feeling confident. After only a couple of hours, she'd gathered together some ideas she thought would go down well and explained them to Tina.

"Shall I dictate this?"

"No, that's fine. I can take it from here," Tina said.

The newsletter was typed up, printed out and placed on her desk in just over an hour. This management lark was a breeze.

The newsletter began,

'Dear cuss homers,

We have sum very special offers coming up in the next too months. Four a start their is stationary at magic prices witch mean it won't stay around long. We have knew medical dairies to keep you informed and too right in all you're sick appointments and animal calendars ewe will love ...'

Sara read through chuckling at the bizarre spelling until she reached the end.

'... hottest regards
Sahara Nesquick'

Tina really did have a great sense of humour. Sara just

couldn't understand why Donald hadn't appreciated her. She took the letter back to Tina.

"Very good, Tina, but I did spot your deliberate mistake."

"Oh, you did? Sorry I couldn't resist. You know it was just a joke, don't you? I know that's not how your name is spelled."

"Don't worry. I can take a joke."

As Sarah spoke, the phone rang. Tina answered it.

"That's head office. They want you to go over for a meeting."

"Fine, I'd better go."

"Shall I put the newsletter right and send it out?"

Sara hesitated. If she said no, it would really knock Tina's confidence.

"That'd be great. Thanks."

Sara was surprised to see Donald at the meeting and didn't dare ask why he was there. He greeted her pleasantly and she in return managed to be polite to him. The bosses made it clear that her position was probationary and she was to maintain the standards set by Donald.

"Of course, thank you," was the only response she could come up with.

Back in her own office, she called the staff together and informed them she expected them to work hard for her. In an effort to put past problems behind them, she suggested they re-arrange the office. The staff weren't enthusiastic, but reluctantly discussed where they'd like to sit and who should have a seat by the window.

To show she wouldn't ask them to do things she wouldn't do herself, she re-arranged her own office too. Once she'd shifted the desk and chairs and swapped the pictures around the place felt less like Donald's office and more her own. She couldn't move the filing cabinet herself and asked one of the lads to help her. He had no trouble shifting it, but did get dust all over his smart black trousers.

Using his hands, he managed to brush most of it off. "Is that all off it?" he asked.

"Turn around," Sara said.

There was more dust on the back of his left knee and Sara flicked it away.

"Oooh, excuse me! Shall I leave you two alone?" the cleaner called from the doorway.

She was gone before Sara could explain.

Two days later, she had another call from head office. She was asked to explain the errors in the customer newsletter.

"Um, sorry, I'll have to call you back."

Sara rushed out to Tina and asked to see the newsletter in her sent box. In horror, Sara stared at the screen as Tina displayed a newsletter not very much better than the one that had made her laugh. It no longer seemed funny.

"You stupid woman, if you can't spell, couldn't you at least look words up in a dictionary?" she fumed.

Sara walked away from Tina before she was tempted to throw her stapler at the girl. As she walked back towards her own office, she tried to think of some way to save the situation. Could she claim it was a new way of gaining customer attention? She was concentrating so hard she'd probably not have noticed Phil asleep at his own desk, if he hadn't been snoring quite so loudly.

What should she do? Someone from head office was probably already on the way over. They wouldn't be impressed with her management abilities if they found her staff asleep. She leant over him and said his name. He didn't stir, so she put a hand on his shoulder to shake him. She stopped almost immediately, wondering how it might look if anyone were to walk in and see her with an arm around him. That's how rumours started. She didn't want to get a reputation, so took a step back and called his name. There was no reaction so she tried again a bit louder. Nothing. Maybe he was ill rather than just taking a sneaky nap.

"Phil! Phil! Can you hear me?"

"Of course I can. What an earth's wrong with you?"

"I thought you were ill …"

"Phil, what's up?" Tina asked as she rushed in.

"I don't know, I was just concentrating on this report and she started yelling at me."

"She did the same to me just now and she called me stupid."

"She never!"

"Did too, but that's nothing compared to what the new cleaner said she did to some poor lad. I didn't believe it at first, but …"

Sara ran to the toilet in tears. How could they think such horrible things about her? She cried for a few minutes until gradually her sobs became a feeble whimper. She blew her nose and tried to pull herself together. It was just the strain of management. All she had to do was keep calm and things would be OK. She checked her reflection in the mirror, removed smears of mascara, tidied her hair and took a deep breath.

She strode down the corridor towards the main office and stopped outside when she heard raised voices.

"We're going to have to do something about Sara," Tina said. "She's even worse than Donald was."

"I've still got copies of those photos of her. What do you reckon head office will say when they find out she blackmailed the boss's son-in-law?" Phil asked.

Tina went back to her desk and telephoned her resignation through to head office. If she acted quickly enough, she might be able to prevent her name being smeared. Maybe if she were to explain to Donald, he'd sympathise and help her get a good reference.

No, probably not. It didn't seem likely that he'd be the only one to have a good word to say about her.

25. A Friend And Colleague

"I feel so sorry for poor Lilly Forrester, she's worked here for years," Franny said.

"Don't worry, we'll give her a really good send off," her boss, Sasha, replied.

"Is that a good idea? She'll be reminded of what she'll be missing."

"I don't think that'll worry her, Franny!"

Franny was only twenty, but felt great sympathy for poor Lilly's plight. Franny would miss more than just her wages if she lost her own job at Invite an Impression printers. Lilly must be dreading retirement. Franny tried talking to her.

"Don't you worry about me, Franny. I'm looking forward to having some time to myself. When I left the college and came here, it was supposed to be part time, but it didn't work out that way."

Lilly had taken early retirement from her previous job. Obviously she'd hated it and gone straight back to work. Now she didn't have that option. Or did she? Franny tried to tell Lilly she didn't have to retire if she didn't want to.

"It's the law, they can't make you go just because of your age."

"Franny, I've worked long enough." She'd smiled ever so bravely.

On Lilly's last day, Franny held her breath as she waited for Lilly's reaction to the party they'd secretly planned. The office was covered with plates of food the staff provided, and wine paid for by Sasha. There were presents too; the radio Lilly said she'd like, flowers and a selection of gift vouchers.

"What a lovely surprise! You've all been so generous," Lilly said. Her voice wobbled and she blinked back tears as she read the messages in her enormous card.

"Speech," someone called. Franny thought it cruel to force Lilly to continue putting on a brave face.

Lilly thanked everyone for their kindness and good wishes. "You've all been so nice to me over the years as well as today."

"You have such a wealth of experience that we've all learned a great deal from you," Sasha assured her.

"Hear hear," the others, including Franny, added. Lilly had done so much for her since she'd started as a Saturday girl at Invite an Impression and she'd enjoyed chatting with the older woman. Franny would miss more than a reliable colleague.

Lilly continued, "I'm now ready to start making friends with people my own age."

Did she mean she'd be moving into a home? In a quiet moment, Franny exchanged phone numbers with Lilly and offered to visit occasionally. It seemed a kind thing to do.

"You call me anytime you like," Lilly had said, almost as though it were Franny who'd be in need of companionship.

Franny called a few days later and suggested meeting up for tea and cakes on her day off.

"Sounds lovely, Franny, but unfortunately I'm busy that day. How about next Saturday?"

Franny readily agreed. Poor old Lilly probably had a

doctor's appointment, or maybe it was pension day. Franny supposed Lilly liked to spread such things out so that, as much as possible, there was something to do every day. Otherwise she might have no reason to leave the house, or even get out of bed.

When they did meet, Lilly talked about having plans.

"Take my advice dear, don't put things off for when you've got time or money. Enjoy life now. Make the most of every minute. If there's something you'd like to do, then start doing it."

"Er, right."

"Do you have any hobbies or interests?"

Maybe Lilly was trying to get suggestions to fill her lonely days? Franny tried to think and remembered Lilly had once mentioned an interest in art. "I've always fancied painting or drawing."

"That's marvellous and it might help with your career," Lilly said.

"I'm not very good."

"You don't need to be good to enjoy it and you'd get better if you practised."

Lilly was displaying the same determined spirit as when she'd first persuaded Franny to apply for a permanent position on reception at the printers. It was good to see she hadn't completely given up on life, Franny thought.

Franny popped round to visit Lilly after work on Monday. Lilly wasn't there.

"She'll likely be up the hospital again," a neighbour informed her.

Franny called on Lilly two or three times a week. Only rarely was Lilly at home. Lilly always said she was well when asked, so Franny didn't like to mention the hospital visits. Instead, Franny caught her old friend up with the work gossip. There wasn't much else to talk about. Lilly would never have anything to talk about, so Franny never enquired. Lilly always asked what Franny had been doing. The girl tried, for the old lady's sake, to make her life seem interesting. It wasn't easy.

On the way home from Lilly's one day, Franny spotted art materials in the window of the charity shop Lilly had told her often had wonderful bargains. On an impulse she bought them and decided she'd use them, then tell Lilly, in the hope the older woman would follow her example.

Franny's next day off was warm and sunny and Lilly had declared herself busy again, so Franny took her art materials to the park. She'd never been there before, but Lilly had said how pretty it was and how friendly the people who used it were. Franny tried drawing a dog she saw. The result was not at all good.

"Is that my dog?"

Franny jumped at the sound of the man's voice. She glanced down at her pad. He must have been judging by the colour of the pencil she was using as there weren't really any other clues. If there'd been a child dressed in clothes the same kind of yellowy brown it could just as easily have been him.

It was no use hiding the drawing as the man had already seen it, so Franny was forced to admit the truth. Normally she'd have been too shy to speak, but there was something familiar about him and he had an encouraging smile.

"I can't actually draw, I just bought this stuff on a whim and then thought I might as well have a try."

"I'm not in a hurry," the man said. "If you like, Jasper and

I will sit here for a bit and you can try again."

"I don't want to put you out."

"That's OK. To be honest, it'll be nice to have someone to chat to. I've not lived here long and I don't know many people." He sat next to her and asked advice on the best food shops, how often the busses ran, when the recycling was collected and similar things that, thankfully, she knew the answers to.

Franny tried again to draw the dog. The second attempt was worse than the first, perhaps because more of her attention was on the owner than the dog.

"I expect I'm putting you off," the man was kind enough to say.

She could hardly admit the truth of that, so said, "I think I need more practise."

"Great. Might see you here next week, then?"

She didn't mention her encounter to Lilly. She was afraid she'd be told not to speak to strangers, or otherwise discouraged from returning to the park the following week. Instead, she suggested Lilly get a pet. Walking a dog seemed a good way to meet people.

"It wouldn't be fair, Franny. I've not enough time to look after it."

How sad, Franny thought; Lilly must only have a few years left.

"Have you tried any drawing?" Lilly asked.

Franny was surprised. She couldn't remember telling Lilly about her recent purchase. "Yes, actually I have. I'm not very good but it's quite fun."

Lilly produced a book on art exercises. "It's very basic. I hope you're not offended, it's just you said you've had no training so I thought this might help."

"Thanks very much." Maybe by the time she'd done the exercises Lilly would be ready to give them a go and Franny could return the book.

Franny practised every evening before her 'date' with Jasper and his owner. She also practised hairstyles and experimented with lipstick. Her new look gave her a little confidence but that evaporated on the way to the park. He wouldn't be there. He wouldn't talk to her if he was. Franny was wrong. Man and dog were waiting to chat and pose respectively, when she reached the bench.

Martin introduced himself and told her she'd been right about the bakery. "Best Belgian buns I've had in years."

They talked about their favourite foods as Franny sketched. The art exercises had helped a bit, but not much.

"You've got his ears almost perfect," Martin said. He was being generous, but at least the drawing was good enough that he could see which bits were supposed to be Jasper's ears.

"All this chat has made me thirsty. Fancy a coffee? The little cafe over there will let us sit outside with Jasper." He didn't really give her a chance to reply, just carried her sketch pad toward the cafe.

When Franny saw Lilly next, Lilly said, "There's a television programme about drawing animals on next Wednesday. Maybe you could record it?"

"Good idea. Actually, I have been trying to draw a dog."

Poor old Lilly, Franny thought. Nothing better to do than watch daytime TV, while Franny got to spend her free time with a good looking young man. She felt herself blush as she recalled the way Martin's hand had brushed hers when he returned her sketch pad. She wanted to confide in Lilly, even seek advice on developing a relationship, but couldn't quite find the nerve.

"I'll see you next week," she said as she got ready to leave Lilly's house.

"I won't be here, I'll be up at the hospital." Lilly spoke quite casually as though it were normal to spend time in hospital.

"Oh, maybe I could visit you?"

"Yes, that's a good idea. In the meantime, you keep practising your drawing."

It wasn't until the weekend that Franny realised Lilly had forgotten to say which ward she'd be on. She didn't have time to call and ask though as she was already on her way to the park to meet Martin and Jasper.

Martin was there, alone.

"Is Jasper OK?" Franny asked.

"He's fine, don't worry. I just thought …" he blushed.

Franny stared for a moment before realising he was shy. She knew how awful that could feel.

"What were you thinking about, Martin?" she coaxed as gently as she could.

"There's an art exhibition on," he mumbled.

"Today?"

He nodded.

"Were you thinking we could go?"

He nodded, more enthusiastically.

"I'd love to."

"Great. If we walk fast, we should catch the 37." He took

her sketch bag and set off at a brisk pace.

Franny followed and jumped on the bus behind him.

"This bus only goes up to the hospital," she told him as he bought their tickets.

"The exhibition is of work done by day care and other long term patients."

"Oh!" Franny said. "I wonder if we'll see my friend Lilly?"

"Lilly Forrester?" Martin asked.

"Yes. I used to work with her. How do you know about her?"

Martin pulled a leaflet from his pocket. It was about the exhibition and named the art teacher and event organiser; Lilly Forrester. "She gave me this and suggested I bring a friend. She's my great aunt."

Thank you for reading this book. I hope you enjoyed it. If you did, I'd really appreciate it if you could leave a short review on Amazon and/or Goodreads.

To learn more about my writing life, hear about new releases and get a free exclusive ebook, sign up to my newsletter – subscribepage.io/ItLSNa or you can find the link on my website patsycollins.co.uk

<u>More books by Patsy Collins</u>

Novels

Firestarter
Escape To The Country
A Year And A Day
Paint Me A Picture
Leave Nothing But Footprints
Acting Like A Killer

Little Mallow cosy mystery series

Disguised Murder and Community Spirit in Little Mallow
Dependable Friends and Deceitful Neighbours
in Little Mallow
Deadly Words and Innocent Gossip in Little Mallow

Non-fiction

From Story Idea To Reader
(co-written with Rosemary J. Kind)

A Year Of Ideas:
365 sets of writing prompts and exercises

Short story collections

Over The Garden Fence
Up The Garden Path
Through The Garden Gate
In The Garden Air
Beyond The Garden Wall

No Family Secrets
Can't Choose Your Family
Keep It In The Family
Family Feeling
Happy Families

All That Love Stuff
With Love And Kisses
Lots Of Love
Love Is The Answer

Criminal Intent
Crime In Mind

Slightly Spooky Stories I
Slightly Spooky Stories II
Slightly Spooky Stories III
Slightly Spooky Stories IV
Slightly Spooky Stories V

Perfect Timing
A Way With Words
Dressed To Impress
Coffee & Cake
Not A Drop To Drink
Making A move
Days To Remember
A Clean Bill Of Health
Your Good Health
Unearthing The Truth